Losing Face

Losing Face

Annie Try

Winchester, UK
Washington, USA

First published by Roundfire Books, 2012
Roundfire Books is an imprint of John Hunt Publishing Ltd., Laurel House, Station Approach, Alresford, Hants, SO24 9JH, UK
office1@o-books.net
www.o-books.com

For distributor details and how to order please visit the 'Ordering' section on our website.

ISBN: 978 1 78099 119 1

A CIP catalogue record for this book is available from the British Library.

Design: Stuart Davies

Printed and bound by CPI Group (UK) Ltd, Croydon, CR0 4YY
Printed in the USA by Edwards Brothers Malloy

For Ken

Tuesday, 12 April

Windows Live Messenger

Em the Gem says:
Hiya Cass – how ya doin?

Cass X says:
ok thanx. Xept for nightmares & panics – u know. ☹

Em the Gem says:
Yeh. I no. I'm still getting them, urs must b 100x worse

Cass X says:
I spose we have 2 live with it.

Em the Gem says:
Jen – social worker, not Jen in PE – a says write it down. Better out on paper.

Cass X says:
I try not to think about it all – just push it away.

Em the Gem says:
yeh – but that makes it worse, doesn't it? I'm going well loopy.

Cass X says:
I'm totally round the bend. Its not much fun, I can tell u.

Em the Gem says:
We gotta do something.

Cass X says:
Agree – but writing will make us think about it.

Em the Gem says:
Jen said u take control.

Cass X says:
How does she know?

Em the Gem says:
I dunno. Jen knows these things. Im gonna try. Can we do it together? ☺

Cass X says:
What meet up & do it?

Em the Gem says:
No. Here or by email.

Cass X says:
What – you write a bit, then me?

Em the Gem says:
Yeh, attachment. Then we can run it off & put it together.

Cass X says:
What for?

Em the Gem says:
Jen reckoned if put tog like a book, I'll feel more tog 2. Should work for u 2.

Cass X says:
I dunno. I'll think about it.

Em the Gem says:
Don't think – just do. Must b better than now.

Cass X says:
There r lots of bits I don't know. Maybe I should face up to it lol! ☺

Em the Gem says:
Lotsa bits I dunno 2.

Cass X says:
ok we'll have a go. Tell me everything.

Em the Gem says:
Write it dead honest then? No covering up?

Cass X says:
ok. No promises mind, cos I'll have 2 start first & don't know if I can. ☹

Em the Gem says:
C if u can. Pls ☺ C u ltr – gotta go. Susie's calling me 4 t. Bye

Cass X says:
Bye 4 now.

That night!! Chapter 1 Friday, 11 April 6.31 PM

From: cassandra briggs [cassab88@yahoo.co.uk]
To: Jennings, Emma
Chapter 1.CB.doc

Hi Em

I've made a start. Here's my first piece. I could've started with what happened earlier and written about that row I had with Mum – or the day before that when Mum's friend told on us – but I think this is the real beginning. I've begun with the night when I made the biggest stupid mistake of my whole life.

It was awful writing it. I felt quite upset and I've had really bad nightmares. I started three days ago. It was the first time I'd really let myself think through what happened.

It feels like putting together fragments. Little fragments of our lives. All those pieces I've been trying not to think about. It's really strange.

Love

Cass x

PS I numbered it 1, like a chapter in a book, so you can do chapter 2.

1

by Cass

I shouldn't have been there that night, really. I don't know if I told you before but my Mum thought I was doing revision for my mock Biology GCSE with Hayley (you know her, the brainy one who never stops talking). Anyway, that's where I said I was going. I had to get out of my house after what my Mum had just tried to 'discuss' with me in a 'mature manner'. I did set off to go to Hayley's, but I reached the end of the road and just stuffed my revision cards into the pocket of my parka and turned left instead of right to go towards your house. Being with you was strictly out of bounds – you remember why! I wish now that I'd been a good girl and gone to Hayley's. Nothing personal, but the way things worked out . . . well, you know.

But there we were, 15 minutes later, with Jackie and Liz, in the Tesco car park. I'm not sure why you said we'd meet the boys there, it's fine in the summer but in December the wind whips across from the fens and it's always absolutely freezing. It was so cold we were clapping our hands together and stomping up and down as if we were at some rave. Then you showed us some dance steps and before long we morphed into a girl group – mimicking your crazy movements and all singing 'Rocking around the Christmas Tree' into imaginary microphones. I don't know what the evening shoppers thought of us.

Despite the cold, I was feeling really excited. Remember how much I liked Spider? Up until that night I'd worshipped him from afar, well, from behind you, I suppose. I was really shy. (Still am, except when I'm singing!)

That night I sensed things would be different. And as soon as he drove into the car park, I knew I was right. We stopped our singing and dancing act and watched him climb out of his motor. For some reason he noticed me – unless you'd already told him I had a crush on him, did you? Spider was so fit, I couldn't believe he would look at me twice – I used to think I was really ugly. What Spider said went, and that night, he smoothed back his beautiful black hair, which always looked tousled before he had it all cut off, and he looked straight down at me with those huge brown eyes. I felt the heat rise up through my body and spread right up into my face. Then he spoke. His voice carried across the car park, loud enough for everyone to hear, like some great announcement,

"Cassie babe, you're with me. Rest of you go with Jock and Adam."

I kept thinking, *Me, me, he wants me,* over and over again.

But I just froze to the spot. All you girls were nodding and smiling – Jackie whispered 'Go for it Cass, go for it.' No way could I get out of this without looking a right idiot, and anyway I really wanted to go. So I stopped thinking about what my Mum would say and slowly sauntered over to him.

I climbed into his motor looking as cool as I could. I was so busy trying to look unfazed that I forgot all about the seatbelt, not that it would have made much difference at that point, I felt too gooey to be able to do anything as practical as clunk-click.

So there I was, sat beside him like the cat who'd got the cream. His car was super clean inside and smelled of new polished leather. I kept my hands on my lap so that I didn't leave finger-prints on the seats. It was great when he was driving us down the A10, he talked really nicely about all sorts of stuff, but mostly about his car. I could hardly answer, I couldn't think what to say. I had to keep controlling this great grin that kept trying to creep across my face. Every now and then he gave me that little sideways smile, you know the one. It was awesome. My heart was beating really fast. I imagined all the places we might be going, maybe the cinema, a night club or even just Pizza Hut, perhaps.

Everything was cool – till we got on the A14. I think you were right behind us then, weren't you? Jock overtook us as soon as we'd gone round the roundabout and onto the dual carriageway.

Spider stopped smiling at me – he just snarled and swore at Jock. Then he put down his foot and we sailed past. No contest really – Spider's motor had all the power. But then you lot caught up and you all waved and managed to overtake us when we were stuck behind a beet lorry. Again, no problem to Spider, he just roared past the lorry and you in one go. I can remember you leaning out of the window, with your hair blowing round your face and your purple lips moving up and down making all those strange shapes – what were you shouting? Do you remember? Your face looked kinda distorted with the wind. It made me laugh. Oh, by the way, that was my *Violet Sensation* lippy, you never gave it back.

It was fantastic waving when we passed you again – exhilarating, powerful. Then Spider put his foot down and the car took off. I was jerked back in my seat as we flew down the road. Must've been doing 90 at least and still getting faster. Really fast. I was laughing at first. Then he didn't slow down and overtook two cars by going into the inside lane. That's when I stopped feeling excited and grabbed the seatbelt, fumbling with it to try to get it fastened. I no longer cared what Spider thought, I was going to wear it. There was something jamming it, I couldn't get it to click. My heart started to pound. I felt sick and dizzy.

"Spider, slow down, please" – my voice sounded feeble, almost squeaky. Spider laughed.

"Spider, slow down, slow down!" I clutched at his arm and he shrugged me off.

"We're just getting going, Babe, hold on tight!"

"Stop being so stupid, just stop it!!"

I was yelling now – shrieking at him. I'd totally given up all thoughts of impressing him – I just wanted out of that car. Now.

"Stop and let me out!!"

Spider laughed again.

"You scared, Babe? That's cute." He turned towards me, reached over and stroked my face. "You're even more beautiful when you're frightened, Babe."

He kissed the ends of his fingers, then pressed them on my mouth. I couldn't have cared less.

"Just concentrate on the road!" I yelled.

Then it happened.

Don't ask me why, but what had been a race, going real fast, turned into a slow, horrific nightmare.

The great curving swerve came first. Spider, turning back to face the road, had seen that we had drifted into the other lane – he grabbed the wheel, yanking the car back too far for the speed we were going at. The right side of the car crashed into the central barrier and bounced off it. We went into a spin. Strangely, I had time to imagine we were on the Wurlitzer at the fair – the lights of other cars creating a dazzling whirling effect. Spider gave up struggling to hold the steering wheel. He was screeching now like a little kid. Then, Em, you'll never believe what he did next –

He closed his eyes.

That's when I went all calm and started to pray. I reached across him and pushed on the steering wheel trying to avoid the side of the car immediately in front of us. It swerved and we got past – I remember a small face turning to me from the back seat, eyes wide open, her silent scream filled with Spider's hollering. With an almighty bump we came off the road and I lost hold of the steering wheel. Spider's souped-up-rubbish-on-wheels shot across the verge and there was this huge splintering thump as we hit something and I shot through the windscreen, sliding across what was left of the bonnet.

The world stopped. Then I was crumpled up on the ground smelling the musty wet grass in the dark, surrounded by all these glistening little pieces of broken glass. The pain in my neck was excruciating, it was hurting me to breathe and there was something gritty in my right eye. As I put my hand up to it, I could feel nothing but wetness – slimy wetness. Then everything was turning, turning, I couldn't focus.

The darkness crowded into me.

Chapters 2 & 3 about calling the ambulance and seeing your Mum

Saturday, 12 April 12.20 PM

From: Jennings, Emma [mailto: ejj9@hotmail.co.uk]
To: cassandra briggs
Chapter2.ejj.doc
Chapter3.ejj.doc

Hi Cass
Reading your stuff was awful! Not ‘cause of how you wrote it. That was cool. Just that it brought it all back.
I’ve done two bits (impressive, eh?). That’s ‘cause when I finished the first one, I realised there was more that happened afterwards that you didn’t know about.
But, before you get reading I’ve got two things to tell you.
1, <u>no way</u> did I tell Spider you fancied him. Everyone knew though, it was that obvious!!!!
2, I chucked that lippy away. Sorry. It brought back too many bad memories. I’ll buy you a new one if you want. Not that colour, mind. It gives me the shudders.
Oh, and the thing you crashed into was some farm machinery.
So here you are. Chapters 2 and 3 of the book that will make us famous! (Ha,ha J)
Luv and hugs
Em xx
Ps I was shouting “slow down you ****** fool,” to Spider.
And Jock sends his best and hopes you are ‘coping and improving’. His words not mine!

2

by Em

I thought you were dead when we pulled up behind you. I jumped out and so did Jock. It seemed to take forever to run round to the front of the car where you were. That nutter Spider had hold of your arm and trying to drag you up. He was shouting "Get up babe, get up!" over and over. Apart from his crazy mind, he was fine. The airbag thingy had popped out of the steering wheel just like it was meant to. He had got out with hardly a scratch. Shame there wasn't one for you.

I started shouting at Spider

"Get off her, leave her. She mustn't be moved. Stop that."

Jock was quieter, more patient with him.

"Come on, mate, let go of her now. She can't get up. We'll get some help. You just leave her there." Then Jock pulled Spider away from you, talking to him all the time. You made some dreadful gurgling noise. That's how we knew you were alive.

With Spider out the way, I sort of went into trying to organise things fast. I pulled my phone out of my pocket, but was trembling too much to use it. Jock took it from me and rang for the ambulance. I knelt by you and listened for your breathing. Your face was downwards, so I was worried you'd suffocate. I couldn't think whether I was meant to turn it or not. My mind was going round and round trying to remember stuff from when I went to St John's ambulance for a bit. Mind you, that was two foster homes ago. I knew I had to see if you were conscious.

"Cass, can you hear me. It's me, Em. I'm here, I'll help you. Can you hear me?"

You didn't reply. Meanwhile, Jock was talking to the ambulance service. We had to do a sort of relay thing with me shouting out what was wrong with you and Jock saying it all again into his mobile. My stomach was turning over that bad I could hardly get the words out. I was shaking all over. Jock's mate Luke came over. He took off his jacket and put it round me. Then he went and got Jackie's furry coat for me to put over you.

You were covered in blood and definitely unconscious. I was that scared, I thought you might bleed to death. Yes, right there in front of us with me having no idea what to do! Your leg was at a funny angle underneath you, and your breathing was awful. It was still gurgly, but rasping too. The ambulance people asked Jock to ask me if there were any bones sticking out. I couldn't see. You were wearing that great long purple hoody-jacket thing under your parka. And jeans. I daren't move you to drag those off. I know you want to know exactly what it was like, so I'll tell you. Everything was just this bloody mess. Literally it was, I'm not swearing here. The ambulance people asked if you had head wounds. I couldn't see any. There was loads of blood coming from somewhere, though.

"Tell them I think it's her face. I can't see – and I'm worried she can't breathe with her face in the mud."

They told me, through Jock, how to gently take your head in my hands. It was difficult because you were right up against the metal of the farm machinery. I managed to turn your head a bit to make sure you got some air. I'm trembling here again as I write this, 'cause that's when I saw your face.

Sorry, Cass, you wanted to know what it was like. I'm not sure I can tell you exactly. I can hardly bear to think about it. I was sick. Right there beside you. Really sick. Jock leant over so he could see you and he went dead white. He looked like he might faint. It seemed ages till I heard him say into his mobile,

"There's not much of her face left, far as I can see, and there's just blood where her right eye should be." That was a fair description, Cass, it looked as bad as that.

I reckon Jock decided there wasn't much we could do for you

once we saw how bad it was. He just came and sat by me, turning me away from you and I leant on him and we both just clung to each other.

Jackie and them wanted to see what you looked like. Jock shouted at them to get away. Then they all went and sat above us on the bank, sharing ciggies. We all just waited, listening to that ghastly noise you were making. I started whispering "please make her all right, please make her all right" over and over again. I was rocking back and forwards like some little kid.

"The ambulance is coming, it's ok Em," said Jock. We both knew it wasn't. I remember looking up and counting stars to try to take my mind off your face. All the time I was listening for your next breath.

It seemed like hours before the ambulance came. Then there was this great bustle of action with people asking me what had happened. I tried to tell them, only we were quite a way off so I hadn't really seen. Jock had slowed right down with Spider driving like such a loony. Then it was Police and I had to say it all over again. The cops told us all to go. They seemed to think we weren't really witnesses as such. By then, the ambulance people had trussed you up on some board thing and hidden your face. Then they put you in the ambulance with Spider who just had a neck collar. Not that he needed it, lucky thing. I asked to go to hospital with you, but there was no room in the ambulance. They said your Mum would be there by the time they arrived, so go home.

Jock was great. He dropped the others back at Tesco's car park. Then he took me back to my foster mum's. When we walked in, she started to throw a wobbly when she saw all that blood over me. Jock just talked her through it and explained it wasn't my fault. 'First on the scene' he said – he sounded like a policeman, you know how solemn he can be. Susie always thinks it's my fault if someone's in trouble 'cause, fair enough, it usually is. I did feel to blame, though. We all encouraged you to go with

Spider. Bad move. Bad, bad move. Sorry, Cass.

Susie made us both a hot cup of tea with loads of sugar. I didn't like tea then, but just holding the warm mug with both my hands felt good. Taking sips seemed to calm me a bit. Jock told her how I'd looked after you. Not that I did much, really, but I was well grateful to him for leaving out the bit when I was sick as a dog. And when I was blubbering like a baby. Susie seemed real proud of what I'd done. After Jock had gone she ran me a hot bath with lavender scented candles and her best bubble stuff. Bit OTT, but nice. I kept thinking about you, Cass. I couldn't stop crying. Not while I had my bath, nor even after I'd gone to bed.

I gotta stop here for a bit, and have a breather. I'll do the next chapter later.

3

by Em

I didn't see you while you were in intensive care. It was relatives only. Your Mum was there 24/7 for the first few days. I think your Dad came from Leeds as well, some of the time.

The suspense was killing me. Jackie phoned and said the rumours at school were flying and they weren't good. I didn't even know if you were going to live. So I waited three agonising days and then went round to see if your Mum was back. That was on the Monday evening

Your Mum opened the door and I said I'd come to see how you were. She just stared at me. Can't say as I blame her. She looked real tired and white. She hadn't got any make-up on. I kept saying 'I'm sorry Mrs Briggs, so sorry'. She nodded then, and opened the door. I hardly dared go in.

Your mum walked into your front room and sat down on the sofa, like I wasn't there. There were Christmas cards on the mantelpiece and windowsill, but apart from that the place was a mess, for her. She's usually right tidy, isn't she? Piles of clothes covered one of the chairs. A plate of egg and bacon sat on the telly. Maybe Carl had cooked it for her earlier. It didn't look like she'd touched it.

I sat there for a while, waiting for her to say something. She was half-lying on the sofa with her legs drawn up under her. Every now and again she did a great big sigh. After a bit I got fidgety, so I went and made us both a cup of tea. It took some time and lots of opening and closing cupboards to find everything. Your mum hadn't even moved when I brought the teas back into your front room. It was ages till she spoke. She was looking down into her mug. Mine was too hot to hold, but she had hers in both her hands.

"Why was she there? I thought she was at Hayley's."

Her voice was flat and slow.

"I don't know. She just turned up on the doorstep and said she'd come to see me." I paused. Your mum looked up, her eyes were blank. She seemed to be waiting for more.

"I was on my way out. Susie wasn't in 'til 9 so I thought I'd go and meet everyone up in the car park for a bit."

"Susie?"

"My foster mum."

"Oh, I didn't know. Cassandra didn't tell me you were fostered."

"I live with Susie. She's on her own, 'cept for her little boy Sam. He's 18 months old and well cute."

She nodded, so I started telling her about the eight different foster homes I'd been in before. But she'd gone all quiet and was staring into her mug of tea again, so I gave up. She did a great long sigh and I wondered whether to leave. But I felt like looking after her, Cass. And you know how scared I was of your Mum before then. Now I didn't like to leave her on her own.

"Where's Carl?" I asked.

Your Mum looked at me like she'd forgotten I was there.

"I think he's gone home, or he may be down the pub."

I was real worried about your Mum, Cass. This wasn't like her at all. I tried asking after you again. This time she replied,

"She's still in the intensive treatment unit."

"How is she?" I wanted to ask whether you were awake, whether you knew where you were, you know, whether your brain was ok. I thought I'd better not.

"The plastic surgeon will see her when she's on the main ward." She looked at me and her face changed. Her eyes went like she was giving me the evils and she said, really quiet and careful:

"She'll never be the same. She will never ever be my beautiful

Cassandra again."

I didn't know what to say.

Your mum put down her tea and put her head in her hands. She was sort of curled over with her elbows on her knees. I wondered if she had started to cry. I didn't know what to do. I began to feel like everything was my fault. I needed to get away. I stood up and started to put on my coat. Then I realised your card was in the pocket. I held it out towards your mum.

"I've got this for Cass, I mean, Cassandra. Would you take it for me?"

She nodded and took it.

"I've got to go now, Mrs Briggs. Can I come back and see you another evening?"

Your Mum didn't even answer me. She looked up, but not at me. She was staring across the room towards that big photo of you that's done like a painting.

I walked back up the hall and let myself out.

I wanted to go and see her again but I couldn't go on the Tuesday 'cause of all that stuff I had to have in for Child Development. It was well overdue. I hadn't even started on my kids' picture book, but Susie knew what was needed 'cause of Sam. So she helped me with deciding how to do it and I drew all the pictures, which worked out quite good. Then I wrote a bit about what I'd done. I had to make it sound like I'd been working on it for weeks, mind. You know, even that appraisal bit looked quite good once I printed it off. Did you know I got a B for that project? I was well chuffed.

Anyway, when I went back on the Wednesday, your Mum opened the door and said

"You again".

She let me in though.

I followed her into your front room and stood there, not knowing what to do. Your Mum stayed standing up too – just looking at me. Made me feel right awkward.

"How's Cass?" I said.

Your mum didn't answer for ages. The room felt like it was shouting what was in my head, which was "talk to me". She did.

"She's not good."

"Oh, I'm sorry."

There was a silence. I wanted to know whether you liked the card, but I was worried about asking. Then I thought if you were real bad you might be dying and you wouldn't even know I cared about you. I had to know.

"Were you able to give her the card?"

"Card? Oh yes, the card. Yes, she saw the card."

"She's conscious then?"

Your mum answered in this really flat voice.

"She opened her eyes and started trying to talk this morning. But the doctor sedated her again, because she needed to be kept still."

Then your Mum told me you had your arm in plaster, your leg all wired up and some broken ribs. She didn't say anything about your face or your eye.

Your Mum looked straight at me and said, very slowly, "They say she's lucky to be alive." I couldn't think of anything to say.

She went a bit quiet then. I made her a cup of tea. I thought she might tell me off today, for taking liberties or something, but she just said "thanks".

We sipped at our tea in silence. Every gulp I made sounded like this real loud noise and that clock of yours on the mantel-piece was ticking like some bomb. Then, finally, when I thought she'd never say anything again, so I'd better just go, your Mum started asking me questions.

"Has Cassandra been round to yours often on a school night?"

"Er, no. Not often. But a few times, maybe three."

"I see. And what do you know about this boy whose car she was in?"

"Spider? Oh, I've known him ever since I came to live here. That's nearly a year. He's at college studying mechanics."

"And did Cassandra meet him often?"

"I don't think so."

"I can't understand why she didn't tell me about him."

I didn't tell her that it was probably because he wasn't your boyfriend or anything, so there was nothing to tell. Wish I had really, that would have been a real good idea, as things turned out. Mind you, if he had been your boyfriend, I don't think you'd have told her. You were too mad with her about Carl wanting to move in.

She carried on asking me stuff and I just kept telling her I didn't know. I didn't want to betray you, Cass. Your Mum didn't give up,

"Where did Cassandra meet Stephen Rider?" she asked. "Was it at your house?"

That put me in a bit of a spot really, so I told her 'no' and that Spider was just a person who was part of the group and we'd bumped into him a few times. I didn't think you'd want her to know you'd been hanging around with all of us in the car park.

"Did you know he is only just 17?"

"No," I didn't know what your mum was getting at – did she think he was the wrong age for you, or what?

"And did you know he hasn't even passed his driving test?"

Honest, Cass, I did not know that, or no way would you have got in that car. Spider's been driving various motors for the past year, so I just assumed he was legit. Anyway, he said he was 19, and 'cause he's at college, we believed him.

I tried to tell your Mum I didn't know, but she wasn't listening, just going on about Spider.

"He's not even learning! Apparently he hasn't even got a provisional licence. What my daughter was doing in his car, I do not know." She was talking real fast and hard. "What he has done to her is diabolical. He ought to be locked up. She will never be the same again. He has ruined her life. And what for?"

I just shook my head. I didn't dare say anything.

"Just to show off!"

She banged her cup down on the coffee table as she said this. Her tea went everywhere. She just sat and watched it dribble onto the carpet.

"I'm real sorry about what happened Mrs Briggs. I hope Cass gets better soon." I knew that sounded pathetic, under the circumstances.

Your mum didn't take her eyes off the dripping tea. She seemed quiet again.

I stood up to go but remembered I'd brought some fruit pastilles, you know, those sugary ones you like. I pulled them out of my coat pocket,

"Please would you give Cass these from me?"

Oh, Cass, it was awful. Your mum just stared at the sweets like they were poison. She turned her head away from me, but not before I saw her eyes glistening with tears. She stood up and picked up the cups, walking back into the kitchen. I was still holding the sweets. I think she was trying to get her act together, because when she came back in the room she told me quite calmly why sweets were 'inappropriate'. I'm sorry, Cass, I had no idea. No-one had told me you had tubes and things to feed you.

I put the pastilles back in my pocket and left.

I love fruit pastilles!! & Chapter 4 Tuesday, 15 April 9.23 PM

From: cassandra briggs [mailto: cassab88@yahoo.co.uk]
To: Jennings, Emma
Chapter 4.CB.doc

Hi Em
Thanks for buying me those pastilles! That was really nice of you. They should've liquidised them and fed them to me down the tube!
I knew my mum must have been fazed by what happened. She was so weird in hospital – well, you'll see, I've written about it in this chapter. I suppose it must have been awful for her. It was really odd the way she was with Spider, though. Sometimes she was really mad with him – like when she spoke to you – and then another time she was extra nice and seemed to be trying to get us together. I'm still not sure what that was about.
Do you know, I think she's even more confused than I am. That's scary, isn't it?
Anyway, here's chapter 4. It's all about my face, a Welshman and a freak show.
Must go – got to do physics revision, I've been sent a mock exam to do at home tomorrow, because I missed the one in January – uugh! ☹
Luv
Cass x

4

by Cass

I don't remember regaining consciousness – apart from a vague feeling of coming back. Like being in a dream and then you're not and then you are again. Even the last few days of those two weeks, when apparently I was with it, are fuzzy now. I can just remember bleeping noises and people bending over me. And the pain – so much pain – coming and going as I drifted in and out of focus. My Dad says your brain is very good at crossing out stuff you can't bear thinking about, but I'm not sure he's totally right. It's not just the pain I can still remember. Going through the windscreen, that's what most of my nightmares were about. And yelling 'stop, stop, STOP!' as we go faster and faster.

Somewhere among all these dreams and things I can remember a really, really bright light. It seemed to be pulling me towards it. It was unearthly, heavenly, comfortable. It made me feel calm. That bit felt more real than a dream.

I know that as I began to understand where I was and what happened to me, so my emotions went all over the place. I was crying a lot, and a lady came to see me a few times and talked really slowly and carefully to me. She asked me how I was feeling and what I was thinking. I just didn't know at that stage. I'd been told my arm and leg would heal ok, and I could see ok with one eye but the other one was all bandaged up. It's strange using only one eye, everything looks the same, but sort of closer. At first I kept reaching out for things, and missing them!

No-one told me for ages that my right eye was so damaged it had been removed. Mind you, Mum's said since that I had to be told several times because I didn't seem to understand. That was the morphine, I expect, or perhaps I didn't want to believe it. But one day when a staff nurse, Sarah, came in to put drops in the good eye, I managed to ask her why I needed them.

"Well, when one eye is damaged or removed, there's a risk of infection in the good one. These drops help prevent it."

"So will I still need them when my other eye heals?"

She sat on the bed and took my hand.

"Cassie, your right eye is gone, remember? It was so badly damaged that it was surgically removed."

I could sort of remember, but that's when it hit me for real. After that I had major problems coping. One minute I was all calm, thinking things like "lots of people have only one eye – they manage fine", then the next minute I felt like my head would explode with the awfulness of it. I was in a right state.

Before, I'd sort of believed in God but if he was there, then why hadn't he looked after me? But maybe he had and that's why I wasn't dead? But what was the point of not dying if I was left like some sort of half-blind ugly misfit? I felt like screaming and crying all at once, I didn't even know if I was glad I to be alive.

Dad helped me loads – you're right, whenever I surfaced he seemed to be there – I don't know what they were doing without him at his work. Although, some of that time was Christmas holidays. Once, I came out of a doze to see Mum and Dad pulling a cracker. Dad laughed, but Mum shushed him. I tried to say something, but I couldn't make myself heard. I wanted so much to hear my Dad laugh.

Then, as the days went on and I slept less and less, Dad would really try to cheer me up. I would hear him stride into the ward, always taking time to have a joke with the nurses and then he'd appear in my cubicle, grinning as he whipped out a surprise from behind his back. Flowers, or a magazine or something strange like a heart-shaped stone he'd spotted in the park. You know, he didn't seem to notice that I looked a mess – it was just Dad, being funny. I felt so much better when he was around.

But, Mum! Oh those two were poles apart. They were like

some strange double act. She would come in and talk to me in a hushed voice, all caring and careful; it was excruciating! Like I was four again or something. I remember one day she and Dad were in the room together, and Dad was messing about telling me some tale. It was about somebody at work, I think,

"Anyway, Cassie, this chap finished telling the joke about the tiny bit of dust and waited for us to laugh. No-one did. So then he said 'Don't you see it?' and we all laughed our heads off."

Mum stood up and rushed round the bed, putting herself between him and me.

"For goodness sake, Joe, can't you be a bit careful what you say around Cassandra, with her in that condition."

"It's all right Mum, it's ok."

"No it's not, Cassandra. I am really sorry your father isn't more thoughtful."

Dad winked at me while she pecked a quick kiss on my good cheek.

I know she was just trying to protect me, but I needed to forget what had happened, not be reminded. I had noticed she was having trouble looking at my face, she seemed to focus on my left ear whenever she spoke to me and she always sat on my left-hand side.

You wanted feelings, so here are some more that I was feeling then. The main one being PAIN. Mostly in my face. I started to long for the painkillers and even once I'd had them, I pleaded with the nurses for more. I had my leg all strung up like in some comic get-well card, because of my smashed hip and leg. It doesn't feel funny, I can tell you! I couldn't move my left arm very well and I felt sore all over. Part of that was because it was uncomfortable to stay in one place, so I got stiff. It was a bit better once the physio girls came and worked on me. They hurt like nothing on earth, but afterwards it helped a bit. You know, Em, I never, ever want to be in a hospital bed again. If I ever have a baby (which I doubt), I shall hide the fact I'm preggers and go and hide in the woods when the labour pains start!

It wasn't long after I was moved to the ward that my plastic surgeon, Mr Mace, came to see me, with Mum. It was awful, Em. He had all those students with him. There was a really tall girl with a beautiful, slightly Asian, face and long dark hair, and a really young one – male – with curly blonde hair. Then there was Sister Trendall and another nurse I knew already and a lady junior doctor. I know what you'd have thought of them, Em. You'd say they were like rent-a-crowd queuing up for a freak show. I felt really vulnerable.

Mr Mace was all right himself, I suppose. He came and sat by the bed and smiled. He held his head on one side as he looked at me – I noticed his eyes were green and he had sandy coloured hair. He smelled really strongly of that hospital handwash, like he showered with it, or something. He held my good hand and talked very slowly to me about how he was going to create an eye socket, repair my cheekbone and rebuild my jaw. Em, I hadn't even seen myself in a mirror before that, so what he was saying seemed crazily unreal! My heart was pounding away like mad and I kept thinking 'this isn't happening to me, THIS IS NOT HAPPENING!!'

"This is a lot for you to take in Cassandra," he said. "I can see it's very hard for you. Maybe I'll just tell you about it again."

His voice was quiet, with a soft, rolling accent, of some sort. Welsh, I think. I tried to concentrate, but I felt sort of detached. What was it that needed so much grafting and reshaping? Could it really be as bad as that?

I pulled my hand out of his and started to touch my face while he was talking. I felt my forehead first – that seemed ok, perhaps a bit swollen. My fingers met the bandage over my eye socket – just below that I felt the rough surface of my cheek. It felt all knobbly and lumpy just below the bandage. I couldn't find the line of my cheekbone. My fingers checked the other side – all fine, but on the bad side it wasn't there. Then I felt a lumpy line down my cheek, and where my jaw should be it just seemed to slope down to my neck. The full horror of it was really hitting me.

The surgeon had a hand mirror, and asked me to look in it while he talked to me. There was no way I dared look in the mirror. I turned my head away from him – desperately wishing I could just get up and run. I was really hot and fighting back the tears. Then I started to take these huge panicky breaths.

"It would be good if we all moved away and let Cassie have some air." I think it was Sister Trendall speaking, "Not you, Mrs Briggs, Cassie needs you, you just stay there." Mum was crying, but she came and took my hand and stroked it – that helped a bit.

Once I was a bit calmer, Mum moved away and Mr Mace sat by me again.

"Feeling better?" he asked.

I nodded.

"I'm sorry this is upsetting you, Cassandra. Perhaps we can find a better way for you? If you can't look in the mirror, may we take a few photos?"

"Photos? What for?" even my voice sounded distorted.

"Just to help you. Some patients find it easier to look at a photo. What do you think?"

I didn't dare think, but I nodded.

That's how I got all those awful pictures taken by the hospital photographer, Em. The ones you saw at my Mum's.

Mr Mace came back later that day with the photos in his hand. I didn't want to look, but first he offered me the one of just my left-hand side. That was ok. Then he gave me the next one, which showed all my face. What I saw made me want to puke. On one side of the face it was me, Cassandra Alicia Briggs, blue eyes, a few freckles, darkish hair and the other side – it was no-one I recognised. Just a mess of a face. I wanted to throw away the photos, or tear them up, but I was frozen, fascinated. I just kept looking at this strange distortion of my face. I felt desperately sick. I moved the picture of my good side back on top of the pile and steadied myself. When I looked at the others again, I was desperately hoping both sides would be the same. Stupid, I know, but that's what I kept thinking. I felt Mum's hand on my arm.

"Are you all right, Cassandra dear?"

I looked at her. She looked quite calm. She had her 'I love you' face on. I nearly asked her why she wasn't freaked out, just looking at me, but then I realised she'd been living with the real thing ever since the main dressings came off, so she was used to it. I asked the surgeon a really daft question,

"Can you make me look like I was before?"

Mr Mace shook his head slowly, as he gently took the photos from me.

"No, Cassandra, but we will do our best to move as close to your old appearance as we can. When we have built up your eye socket, the ocularist will have you fitted with a prosthetic eye."

"A glass eye?" My voice had gone all squeaky. The only person I had ever known with a glass eye was the piano tuner we used to have. One eye looked ok but I can remember his glass one staring forward blankly, sticking out further than the other. I must have been about 6, I suppose, and I was very frightened by that eye.

"No, probably not a glass one, most are made of more light-weight materials these days. The implant you have at first will eventually take the customised lens that will be your new eye."

I was swallowing fast. I felt really panicky. I closed my eyes – 'God, help me cope, God, help me cope' was going round and round in my head. As I began to calm down, I could hear Mr Mace was talking again.

"Cassandra – let me reassure you about the eye. It will be designed specially for you to totally match your other eye"

My mother asked, "How do they get it to match?"

"It will be hand-painted, and should look as beautiful as the good one."

It's funny, Em. But I began to feel a bit better – they knew what they were doing with my eye. I sort of lost sight (ha,ha) of the fact that this carefully constructed eye wouldn't see or move. But I felt more in control. There was a moment of quiet while Mum and I watched Mr Mace scribble notes in his file. His face was wrinkled in concentration. I started to think of this man, the surgeon, as someone on my side, working to help me – less of an enemy. He looked up and realised I was watching him.

"Is that enough for today, Cassie, or do you have any questions?"

"What about repairs to the rest of my face?"

"I'm afraid that will be a long job, with lots of surgery. It will take many bone and skin transplants to reshape it. We won't be able to do it all at once, I'm afraid."

I knew really, of course, if I dared think about it. I nodded and turned my face away from him. Then I pulled the duvet over my head. I wanted to bury my face in the pillows, but even that simple thing was not an option with my leg strung up.

As they both moved away, I could hear the murmur of Mum and Mr Mace discussing me. I put my hands over my ears. I'd had enough.

I wished I were dead.

School and stuff Chapter 5 Wednesday, 16 April 5.03 PM

From: Jennings, Emma [mailto: ejj9@hotmail.co.uk]
To: cassandra briggs
Chapter5.ejj.doc

Hi Cass
I read your last chapter. Then I sat up half the night writing my next bit. Well nearly all of it. I finished it when I got in from school today. I think I've remembered everything. It's mostly about school, questions and a bit about Jock. You talking about Mr Mace being Welsh made me wonder if Jock is Scottish. I don't think he is though. Do you? I think he used to live up North somewhere. That's what his accent sounds like, anyhow.
When I read your chapter it made me really think. It must have been the pits, Cass. Bit random, but it reminded me of the day when I was taken into care. That was like the worst point of my life ever. It made me feel awful, like you've written. But I won't go into all of that stuff. It's not really part of what we're meant to be writing about now. You know, to get rid of our nightmares and things.
What I've written here is out of time order. That's cause I'd been back at school for a bit by the time you saw your surgeon. My chapter starts with the day I went back.
I'm feeling down today. I'm trying to sort myself out. Probably it's because of the maths – my mock exam marks were awful. I don't know.
See you after the exam tomorrow.
Luv and hugs
Em x

5

by Em

It was the Tuesday after the accident that I went back to school. I had wanted to stay home for the rest of the term, until Christmas, but Susie made me go. I arrived a bit late for registration. I tried to slide into my seat near the door without being noticed. Fat chance, the whole class turned to look at me. Mrs Styles was trying to take the register, but she had to get almost everyone to listen by repeating their names. Lots of people were whispering 'Is she all right?' and 'Have you seen her?' In the end Mrs Styles clapped her hands and said:

"Right, I can see that no-one is interested in registration until they have heard about Cassandra. Emma, perhaps you would stand up and tell the class, so that we can get on."

Well, you know, I didn't actually have much idea because your Mum hadn't been very talkative. But I stood up anyway and said

"What do you want to know?"

Stupid question – all the class wanted to know different things. Mrs Styles had to make them ask me one at a time. People were really bothered about you, Cass. Once I told them that you were a) still alive and b) going to stay still alive, they asked about your injuries. I told them about your leg, arm and ribs but I couldn't really tell them what they wanted to know about your face. 'Cept you were being tube fed. Then someone said,

"Is her Mum all right?" so I just said she was very upset, as expected. Then Jock asked when you could have visitors – which I didn't know. It was Polly who asked if you needed anything. She got a glare from Miranda for that – what is it about Miranda? She doesn't like you, does she? Anyway, when I couldn't think of anything you'd want, Polly said she'd send a card.

Then Mrs Styles said it was enough questions and I sat down. Then I went all shaky. I kept thinking of you with all that glass round you and that blood. Each time I tried to think of something else, it just popped back into my mind. It felt like I was really there.

It was like that all morning – people kept asking me questions, just as I had stopped thinking about it for a bit. Then the whole thing came back into my mind. I kept thinking *I should have done something, I should have stopped her getting in the car. It should have been me.*

After lunch, I got told off three times in Chemistry, for not listening. So, in the end I went and told Mr Jackson that I felt sick – I did by then anyway. He said I could go out of class for a bit. Mrs Styles was walking down the corridor

"Are you all right, Emma? You look rather pale."

I told her I wasn't feeling too good and she asked me if I wanted to go home. I did desperately want to go back to Susie's. Then I thought. I didn't reckon I'd be able to stop thinking about things wherever I was. Anyway, it was nearly time for Child Development. I was worried about the next project thing we had to do. It was nearly due in and I'd already had an extension on the last one.

Mrs Styles looked a bit surprised when I said I'd manage. I did get through the rest of the day. Only by telling people I couldn't talk about it all anymore, mind.

When I came out of Child Development, Jock was outside. He came and walked by me.

"You all right, Em?"

"Sort of. Can't take these questions, you know."

"Come on then, let's get away before the crowds."

We rushed out the gate and round the corner. I was wearing the wrong shoes for running really – you know, my black boots with the heels. I could hear I was making this clacketting noise on the pavement. We must've looked really odd, getting away like that. By the time I stopped because I'd run out of breath, we were both laughing. Then I felt guilty and sort of sobered up.

"You can laugh, you know," said Jock. "It won't affect what happens to Cass."

He knew exactly what I was thinking.

"I feel so guilty." I blurted out.

"It's not your fault, Em. That maniac Spider shouldn't have driven like he did. All we can do now is support Cass and help her to cope with whatever comes."

I really struggled to say it, but I needed to talk to someone.

"She'll never be the same." I said, thinking of what your Mum said.

"She won't look the same, but she'll still think the same and want the same things and all of that stuff."

I didn't know if you would, Cass. And I didn't know if you'd want a friend who ruined your life. I couldn't hide from Jock that I'd started to snivel like a little kid. Second time I'd cried in front of him.

"Come on," said Jock, "I may as well walk back with you now."

NOT YOUR FAULT! Here's chapter 6

Thursday, 17 April 8.40 PM

From: cassandra briggs [mailto: cassab88@yahoo.co.uk]
To: Jennings, Emma
Chapter 6.CB.doc

Emma Jennings – you silly moo!
Of course I still wanted you as a friend. Anyway, Jock was absolutely right. It was not your fault. In fact, IT WAS NOT YOUR FAULT. (Do I have to spell it out?) Who chose to get in that motor? Was it you? No, it was me.
Anyway, this is chapter 6. As you can see (!) it's about the eye – so you don't have to read it. I know you find eyes a bit difficult.
Love
Cass

PS No nightmares for three nights. Might be because I'm not sleeping, though. Too worried about the thought of coming back to school!
PPS Got a bit upset earlier. Looked at school newsletter on email and there's loads about the prom. I don't think I'll be going now.

6

by Cass

Mr Mace came back on the ward the next day. He popped his head round the door of the cubicle and saw my Mum and Dad – they were both there, trying to be polite to each other because of me.

"Ah, both parents, excellent. Can I have a quick word?"

I was a bit miffed by that. It was my face, after all. But perhaps he just wanted to make sure that they knew what he was going to say so that they could be all shocked and upset before he told me.

Anyway, it was definitely more than one quick word because they took 22 minutes over it. I was really worried that he might have decided I couldn't have any operations and no eye would fit my disfigured face so I would look like a freak that people would run away from. Then I started to think about all the people who have been born with something wrong with their faces, and how they would cope, and whether it was easier for them because they had never known anything different. Perhaps harder, because they would grow up with people pointing. Would people point at me when I got out of hospital? I worked myself into a real state. I was going all hot and cold and feeling very scared by the time my parents and Mr Mace reappeared.

"Sorry to keep you waiting, Cassie, it took a bit longer than expected to talk to your parents because they wanted to ask so many questions."

"About what?" I asked, not meaning to sound as rude as it did when I said it.

"Your surgery. I want to take a bit of your shinbone to build up your eye socket, and although you have the final say about whether it is done, I always think it's best to tell parents first so that they are properly equipped to help you make your decision."

My decision? I'd only just persuaded Mum to let me have a clothing allowance so that I could choose my own clothes and now I was expected to decide whether or not I had a bit of bone cut out from one place to go in another. I was horrified. I must've been gaping at him.

"I'm sorry, Cassie, have I just given too much information in too short a time? My fault. Shall I go over it again?"

I nodded and he told me in more detail what he needed to do.

Mum kept interrupting

"He needs to do it, Cassandra, to take the new thing."

"Eye, Mum. He needs to do it to fit a false eye." She looked like I'd punched her, and I was sorry for a moment, but I knew I had to get my mind round this – strange though it was. Something was going to be fitted into my face to look like I had an eye. More to please others than me. So that I looked better to them. And now I knew it would cause me pain and injury somewhere else to do it.

"You'll have to have it done, Cassandra. You'll look so much better, and you'll feel better, too," said Mum.

"I will never look the same, Mum." She flinched again. I hated this.

"Dad, tell her. I think she thinks it will all be all right if I have this operation."

"Cassie, it's good that you are thinking about all this," said Mr Mace, "but I don't think your mother is quite ready."

I knew that, but Em, I did not want to hear it. If your Mum can't cope it feels really wobbly. Dad had been very quiet up 'til then, but now, thank goodness, he spoke,

"Cass, dear, you will always be my beautiful daughter, whatever you look like. It's the same for Mum, but she's always taken a bit longer to adjust to change. Remember when you went to secondary school?"

I did – Mum walked up to meet me from my old school when I started my first day at secondary. It was only when she got there that she remembered that I would be coming back on the bus. I nodded, Dad went on.

"Mr Mace would like to do your operation in the next week, if you agree to it, so you and I can work out together the best course of action. He will work with the eye surgeon and they can put in your implant ready for your eye at the same time."

Mum was sitting with her arms crossed tightly, her mouth firmly closed as if trying not to say anything. Dad glanced at her and back at me. We both knew that she'd want to make decisions, not leave them to me. I turned to Mr Mace

"When will I meet the prosthetics person – you know, with the false eye. No – I don't mean he's got a false eye. I mean . . ."

I just couldn't say 'Who will talk to me about my false eye.'

"In about five minutes, I should think, he's on a paediatric ward talking to a young lad now, he'll see you next."

It's funny, Em, but when you've had something like this happen to you it feels like you are the only one. This was the first point at which I realised that there was someone else needing a false eye, on a children's ward, so they must be about my age or younger.

"Can I meet him?"

"Well, yes, as I said, he's coming to you next."

"No, I mean the boy."

"Well, I expect so. Talk to Mr Keen or the nurses, they will probably arrange it – but it will have to be today, I think Matt is on the list for surgery tomorrow."

I didn't see Matt that day, because Mr Keen came. Mr Keen definitely lived up to his name. I got the giggles while I was talking to him, because I kept thinking of those Mr Men books we had when we were kids. I don't think there was one for a Mr Keen, but if there was, it should have been about that eye person.

He strode into the cubicle. Pulled over a chair and sat down by me, holding out his hand.

"You must be Cassandra." He announced.

"Yes." I couldn't disagree with that.

"Let's see, yes, I see." He peered at my good eye. He was smiling.

"A lovely hue, lovely hue. I will enjoy creating a match for that. Has anyone told you what I do?"

I told him what Mr Mace had said, and how I was expecting an implant first.

"Ah yes – the implant. You will feel better with something there. It has to go in now to keep the shape of your socket. It's not your final eye, though."

"I know, Mr Mace warned me."

"Would you allow me to demonstrate the difference? I have some examples here."

From his briefcase he took a black leather box. He explained before opening the box that they were for "demonstration purposes only". The box was full of eyes, all carefully embedded in purple silk. He handled each one delicately, carefully, as if they were diamonds. They made me shudder – but when he passed me one, I took it. It was very smooth. It was just a lens – a bit like a contact lens but bigger and harder. As I handled it, I found I was thinking it looked quite good.

"It feels like glass." I said, thinking Mr Mace had got it wrong when he said they weren't glass these days.

"It's actually toughened acrylic, painted. It fits over the implant, in your eye."

"So the implant bit is permanent, then?"

"Oh yes, we will attach it to your own tissues. We might even be able to utilise muscles, to give your eye some movement."

"You can make it move?" For the first time, I began to believe it might look like a normal eye.

"We hope to – we will see how your muscles are. Let me show

you this."

He passed me a photograph of an eye and then took out a matching lens-eye thing from the black box. He placed it on some sort of stand, over a transparent ball, then put a shield with an eye shaped hole over it.

"Now this is one I made earlier – do you think it's a match to my patient's good eye?"

It was – from a photograph, there was no difference. The colours were exactly right. Even the fine lines in the iris were there.

"It's really good. How do you do this?" I asked.

"Well, my dear, it's a work of art. Very delicate painting with very well selected colours."

"Well, this one is a real success."

"And so will yours be, Cassandra. For you we will create a masterpiece."

I became aware of my mother, sitting frozen in the far corner of the room. I don't know when she arrived. She hadn't asked any questions, and now she was fixing her gaze high up on the opposite wall.

"Mum, do you want to see these eyes?"

"Um, not now. Your Dad and I will talk to Mr Keen later." Her voice was shaking slightly. I think Mr Keen noticed. He put everything away and closed up his leather box.

"Well, Mrs Briggs, let's pop along to the nurses' station and arrange a time when you and Mr Briggs can be here together. If that's all right with you Cassandra?"

"Yes, thank you."

Mr Keen shook my hand before he left. I noticed his hands were small and smooth. Just right for painting tiny things.

Squeamish – what me??? Saturday, 19 April 11.09 AM

From: Jennings, Emma [mailto: ejj9@hotmail.co.uk]
To: cassandra briggs
Chapter7.ejj.doc

Hi Cass
I did read your last chapter. Even the bit about Mr Keen and the eye. It was ok. I know I'm a bit squeamish sometimes when you touch your new eye, sorry. It's only because I hate having anything in my own. I can't imagine what all that must have been like for you. I've started to appreciate my sight now. I used to never even think about it.
Anyway, here's my next chapter. I ought to call it Jock, Jen and the chocolate cake, or something! It's a bit rough 'cause I just wrote it real fast.
Luv and hugs
Em x
PS I'll be round l8r if that's ok. I want to show you what we bought at the weekend.☺
PPS Only two days till you're back in school!

7

by Em

Something odd was going on in my head. I was trying to do my schoolwork (for the first time ever!). But I couldn't get my thoughts together. And I was getting screwed up about ordinary things that never bothered me before. You know, like where I sat in class. I missed you, 'specially in school. Even when we weren't in the same lessons, meeting up at breaks and lunchtime brightened things up.

Jock helped a bit. I think it was just his way to be kind. I don't know. Anyway, I'd be feeling all down and forcing myself to do stuff and forgetting random stuff (even to eat my lunch one day!). Jock would just catch up with me after school and start walking with me.

"Hi Em – any news?"

He always started our conversation asking after you, so I would sort of tell him whatever I knew. It wasn't usually much. Then we'd maybe start to chat about other things. I even found myself telling him about my mum. You know, how she had to give me up because of drugs and stuff. And how horrid contact visits are.

Mind you, I thought he must fancy you. He seemed desperate to come and see you. In a way, I was too. I needed to know you were ok.

Susie saw I was a bit mixed up so she made sure I did loads of things with little Sam. He usually cheered me up. He didn't, so she went to plan B, which was to get my social worker round. That's Jen – you've met her, haven't you?

Jen turned up one Wednesday. I like it when she comes because she usually takes me out somewhere. We have something to eat and chat a bit. It used to always be MacDonalds when I was a little kid, but these days it's somewhere more upmarket. Sometimes in Ely. This time we went down by the river in The Maltings and sat in those sofas they've got near the entrance. Jen bought us a huge slab of chocolate cake each and I had a hot chocolate with extra cream. 'Comfort food' Susie calls it. I sure felt like being comforted.

"How are you coping after Cass's accident?" That's another thing I like about Jen, she comes straight to the point. Sometimes we start with making a list of what we are going to talk about. Then we don't forget anything.

"Not good." I said, my mouth full of cake.

"What exactly do you mean by not good"

"I can't get it out of my mind. Well, sometimes I can, but sometimes I can't. And I feel guilty."

I knew she'd say it, and she did.

"It's not your fault, Em."

"That's what everyone says. But if I hadn't been her friend it would never have happened."

"If she hadn't been your friend, she may have been Jackie's. She'd have still liked Spider and most probably ended up in his car."

"Yes, but I seem to always get it wrong. It's like I start something and it rolls out of control."

"Em, did you take Cass to the car park with the intention of her having a ride with Spider and being involved in the crash?"

"No," I spluttered, through my mouthful of cake, "of course not! If I could have done anything to stop the accident, I would have done."

"Then why are you feeling guilty? You can't stop things happening that are out of your control."

She was right, wasn't she? It did make me feel a bit better. But you know, Cass, I still felt a bit scared about seeing you. It was bad enough with your Mum – who just seemed to get upset whatever I said. I was dead worried I would upset you

Jock had been pestering me to arrange a time to visit you. I kept putting it off. But after talking to Jen, I rang your Mum and asked if we could go. .

The chapter about strangers in my room

Tuesday, 22 April 9.53 PM

From: cassandra briggs [mailto: cassab88@yahoo.co.uk]
To: Jennings, Emma
Chapter 8.CB.doc

Hi Em
You know, I might not have coped with seeing you before you did come and visit in hospital. I had an awful lot of stuff going round in my mind – and then there was Mum, who was finding it all a bit much.
Great to see you last night. That jewellery would look perfect with a prom dress when you've found one (no – I'm still not coming, before you ask!). Where will you buy yours? I can't believe Miranda's dress cost £400. Do you think it really did or is she just trying to be the richest girl in school again?
It was really odd seeing everyone at school yesterday. I know it will never be the same, but I am sort of glad to be coming in for a few lessons now.
Anyway, here's the next chapter. I wrote it last night after you'd gone. Please don't take offence. It's the bit about certain people coming to visit, while I was still on the ward – in that side room they call a 'cubicle'.
If you are still talking to me after reading this, are you coming round Friday?
Love
Cass

8

by Cass

I was half-asleep when you arrived.

"Hi, Cass."

Your voice seemed to come from far way. I struggled to pull myself up into a sitting position and turned to face the door. I could just see you beyond the vase of nearly-over roses, bowl of browning fruit and pile of old Christmas cards. You were peering uncertainly round the door. I pulled my hair over to try to cover my face and the eye-patch.

"Can I come in," you asked.

"Oh, uh, sure, yes."

"I've got Jock with me."

"Oh."

"It's ok Cass – he was there, he saw you."

I felt exposed. An ugly monster pirate on full show. I could cope with you – I thought you'd be fine – but Jock, I hardly knew him. He spoke.

"I really wanted to see how you are, Cass. But I'll go if you'd rather."

You and Jock stood watching, by the door. But, Em, you looked away as I caught your gaze. I felt awful, betrayed. I felt like I hated you.

"You've seen me now," I said, and pulled the covers up, hiding my face as much as I could.

You weren't giving up that easily.

"Cass, Jock means he wants to know if you're ok, you know."

I wanted to scream. I wanted to shout 'No, I'm not ok. I have half a face and no eye. Stop gawping!' But the anger drained away – I guess I was too tired and fed up to fight. I gave in.

"All right. You'd better come in."

You both crept into the room. Jock moved the chair closer to the bed for you to sit on, then fetched the other one that was over by the basin. He put it by yours – then you both sat on the edge of your chairs, looking all round the room, but not quite looking at me. I had no way of moving further from you.

"I've brought you some grapes, Cass, and loads of fruit pastilles."

"Thanks."

"We're all missing you at school," said Jock.

"Yes, we're certainly missing you."

It went quiet. I couldn't think of anything to say to you strange people from my past (sorry Em, that's how it felt). It was better when Jock said he'd buy us all a drink from the machine and left us on our own.

"Cass, how are you really coping?"

Do you know, you were the first person who asked me that, except for that psychologist woman. Everyone else told me I must be feeling this, or must be feeling that.

"I don't know, Em. Good days and bad days, I suppose. Although the good days are pretty bad."

"I don't know how to say this Cass, but I am really, really sorry. I should've stopped you getting in that car."

"Don't blame yourself. I should've stopped myself from getting into that car. I just felt embarrassed to say no in front of everyone. You know what it's like."

That's when you told me about getting into a fight with Miranda and all the others gathering round and egging you on so that you couldn't stop fighting because of what they'd think. I couldn't believe it, I'd never seen you fight anyone. Shouting, yes, just a few hundred times, but physical fighting, no!

"What did she do that was so awful?" I asked.

"Oh, you know how it is, I can't really remember what started it all now."

You were lying, Em. You never forget things like that. I knew then it must be that she'd said something gross about me. Miranda had hated me ever since I won that music trophy for singing. She was sure it was going to be hers because of being the lead singer in that band, Skoolzover, or whatever they called it. But I didn't really want to think about Miranda. I changed the subject.

"Are you and Jock an item, then?"

"I wish," you said. "He's well cool. He was great when we were waiting for the ambulance. He really helped, Cass."

I shuddered. I felt exposed again. Even Jock knew more about how I had looked than I did. I wondered if everyone at school was talking about the accident. I didn't dare ask you.

Jock came back, the machine having swallowed his money and produced no drinks. He joked about that for a bit, and we shared fruit pastilles instead. Then you both told me about things that were happening in school, but I'd had it really for the day, and couldn't focus on what you were saying. I think you noticed because you didn't stay long.

Creepy, crawly spider Thursday, 24 April 10.07 PM

From: Jennings, Emma [mail to: ejj9@hotmail.co.uk]
To: cassandra briggs
Chapter9.ejj.doc

Sorry Cass – couldn't resist that title! He did seem a bit creepy – you'll see why when you read chapter 9.

You were right Cass. Miranda did say something about you – well it was two things that upset me really. First she said you'd have to go to a special school – stupid ignorant cow – then, when I put her right on that, she started saying you'd have to drop music GCSE because you wouldn't be able to do your song for the performance. She seemed well pleased about it. I got even madder then.

The fight did just start off as shouting at each other, but then she shoved me and I pushed her back. And then I got real mad with her and sort of punched her, then everyone watching cheered and so I just carried on. Hitting and getting hit. Luckily we'd stopped by the time Miss Tibbetts got there. We both got three detentions though.

I'm sorry I upset you when we visited in hospital. I was worried about looking at you in case you thought I was staring. And I felt really upset about your face. I wasn't really prepared for what you'd look like. It's much better now, isn't it?

See you in school – I am so pleased you are back!

Luv and hugs

Em

9

by Em

You have forgotten something about that day of our visit. Spider turned up just as we were going. That made the atmosphere even more strange. He'd brought you some roses – pink, not red – and he was all charming. He acted like he owned the place.

"Don't mind me you guys, I'll just sit over here till you go." He moved a few of your things to make space, then sat on the windowsill. The window was quite high, so he was looking down on us.

I could see Jock was positively bristling just at the sight of him. He was clenching and unclenching his hands and his jaw looked all tight. I wasn't sure what to do.

I didn't want to leave you, Cass. I know you still thought Spider was all right but I was worried that he wanted to finish you off as a witness, or something. Just my crazy imagination, I s'pose. You didn't say much to him, apart from 'hi' and 'thanks' for the roses, but then you were ready to doze again.

"She needs to go to sleep, Spider. Why don't you come and have a drink in the canteen with us?"

Spider shrugged and said,

"Bye, Babe, see you later." Then he picked up your hand and gave it a great big slurpy kiss. I don't know if you even realised. It made me want to puke.

I don't think Jock was too pleased that Spider was coming to the canteen with us, but he tried to be polite. When we all fetched our cokes and found a table, I started to talk to him about you and your injuries.

You know what he said? I couldn't believe my ears!

"Yes, she's sure lucky to be alive, isn't she? She came off better than the car."

The grossness of what he'd just said must've been written all over my face. But he didn't stop. He went on to talk about you not having your seatbelt on, and all that saved him was that he was wearing his. I now know from what you've told me that the passenger seatbelt didn't even work!

Jock was well rattled.

"What are you doing here, Spider? Why are you hanging around Cass?"

You know how Jock and Spider used to be real good mates? Well, they weren't anymore. Jock's voice sounded real hard when he spoke to him.

"I've got every right," said Spider.

"You've no right, after what you've done!" Jock's voice was loud, well loud. People were beginning to look at us. Spider just looked confused.

"But Cassie is my girl," he said.

Jock and I looked at each other.

"Since when?" I asked. "She's only had one car ride with you and look what happened! It's not what you'd call a long-term relationship."

"But we've been through stuff together. That makes you close. She's my girl now."

"Have you discussed this with her?"

"No need to, Babe, no need. A girl like Cassie, she knows who she likes."

He paused, he was smirking. Proud of himself.

"Anyway, I get on with her mum. I'm well in there."

I doubted it. I reckoned your Mum only put up with him 'cause she thought he and you were an item.

Jock was muttering stuff under his breath. Then he stood up and pushed back his chair. He put his face right down near Spider's.

"You stupid fool. You've no idea what you've done, have

you? You've ruined her life."

Spider just shrugged.

"Cassie will be all right. She'll have a few ops and they'll sort her out. She'll get better." But there was something in his voice that made it sound like he was trying to convince himself. That's when I wondered if he was quite bothered about you, in his arrogant way.

He might even have been sorry. I know he wouldn't admit it, but who knows what Spider really thinks?

Nil by mouth – chapter about the op

Friday, 25 April 6.35 PM

From: cassandra briggs [mailto: cassab88@yahoo.co.uk]
To: Jennings, Emma
Chapter 10.CB.doc

Hi Em

You know, it's really helpful getting all this down on paper. I've got loads of gaps. I couldn't remember Spider being there when you were at all. It was strange about him – the nurses all loved him even though they knew he'd been driving. Sometimes he looks quite young and innocent, so they probably wanted to mother him. I don't know. Come to think of it, I didn't even know what I thought about him. Sometimes it was absolutely awesome that I had someone as fit as him hanging around and saying he was my boyfriend, other days I just hated him.

Anyway it's my turn to write, so I've done a chapter about the op. I've left out all the gruesome bits – so even you should manage to read it!!

Bye for now – c u l8ter!

Love

Cass

10

by Cass

When I woke up that day and I knew I was going to have surgery, I felt really calm. I remember running my fingers over my face and around the edge of my bandaged eye, feeling all those bumpy scars, and thinking "time for change – time for improvement" or something optimistic like that. Anyway, I felt really positive.

My mother, on the other hand, was a wreck! I suppose she had signed those awful consent forms. I was surprised I didn't have to, seeing as how they needed me to consent as well. And they spent loads of time trying to get my views on things I didn't know enough about.

Mum was there when I first woke up that morning and she started fussing immediately.

"Now then Cassandra, remember you can't eat anything. In fact, I don't think you can even drink anything. I can't remember. I'll have to find a nurse."

"Wait Mum, look."

Above my head it said 'Nil by Mouth' – I'd seen the nurse write it before I went to sleep last night.

Mum sat down by the side of my bed, fidgeting about on the brown vinyl chair so that she made little, rather rude noises. It made me smile.

"What's so funny?" she asked.

"Nothing Mum, it's just the noise you're making."

"I didn't say anything. You're imagining things now."

She was twisting her hands and fiddling with her rings. I decided to keep quiet. But she was making me nervous. I reached for my book – reading it was a good distraction. It helped me to shut off from everything that had happened and forget that things would never be the same for me.

Mum cleared her throat a few times. I looked up from my book.

"Are you just going to pretend nothing is happening?" she said.

"What else can I do? I'm going to have an operation – I don't see any point in getting wound up about it."

"That's not like you – you used to be really nervous about things like this, before . . ."

Her voice trailed off and I shrugged and turned back to my book. She was right. I had changed. When something so out of control has happened to you, you sort of give up being worried about the other things. Not that an operation is just nothing, but at least I knew that people were trying to help me. I'd prayed about it and I knew that at least I could put my faith in their skills – it wasn't like some crazy swerving car.

I'd read about three more chapters when breakfast arrived. I pointed to the 'Nil by Mouth' and the girl said 'Oh, sorry, so sorry' and took back the plate she had just put down and backed away out of the door again.

Mum was furious. It kept her busy for a while as she ranted and raved about the left hand not knowing what the right hand was doing and surely they knew that if I ate I would be at more risk from the anaesthetic and on and on. I was really pleased when Mr Mace appeared.

"Well, are you ready for this?" he asked.

He was smiling, and sort of twinkly. Nice. It struck me that he liked doing this as much as I liked singing. It was his thing – his special talent.

"I'm looking forward to it!" I said.

Mr Mace grinned.

"Good for you – I will do my very best for you!"

Everyone started bustling around. The nurses came and put a

cannula in my hand – you know one of those things with pipes ready for medication to come down a tube or whatever. Then they helped me to get into one of those gross gown things that doesn't do up at the back, then the anaesthetist came and I had a chat with him. Then it was brakes off the wheels on my bed and porters wheeling me down the corridor. The first time I'd been off the ward. I remember thinking that the polystyrene ceiling tiles looked tatty and old-fashioned. I tried to talk to Mum about them, but she was somewhere a bit further behind the bed. I could hear the click clack of her best navy heels as she tried to keep up. Then we were in the lift – Mum took my hand then, and I noticed her face, white and strained. Her lips were trembling very slightly. I gave her hand a little squeeze and she tried to smile. Then we were out again on a different floor and into another room, a bright room. There the anaesthetist appeared again, popping up as if by magic. I did start to feel nervous then, but I still had this strong sense of doing right – moving forwards.

The injection he gave me through the cannula felt cold as it started to go in. Then I struggled against the feeling of going, trying to hang on to the sensation of my mother holding my hand.

Apparently the operation took 5 hours. It was unremarkable in that Mr Mace knew what he was doing and did it. No major problems. When I came round, I had no idea where I was, but Mum was there and so was Dad. My face felt tight and uncomfortable – it hurt and so did my leg. I tried to drift back to sleep.

There seemed to be loads of nurses around – all speaking in hushed voices. One of them asked me if I had pain – I was almost too sleepy to answer and anyway my mouth just didn't seem to move as I expected it to. I tried to nod. I tried to move my hand, to beckon her closer but there seemed to be pipes stuck in it, when I tried to pull them out, my mother took my other hand in hers. The nurse was still there – I'm not sure what she did, but it felt a little better almost immediately. The rest of the day was lost as I dozed and came round, then dozed again.

I was still in intensive care when I woke up next morning. Dad was asleep in a chair by me.

"Hi Dad."

He stirred and then jerked awake.

"Cass – are you all right? Is anything the matter?"

"I'm ok, I think. At least I can say something. My throat is really sore, though."

"That's because you had pipes down there – no you haven't any there now."

He was smiling as my left hand had gone up to feel my neck. The right hand still had the cannula stuck in it with tubes – much like last time I was in the intensive treatment unit.

"Do you know what this is for?" I asked him, lifting my right hand.

"Only painkillers – you're doing fine otherwise."

"What does my face look like?"

"I don't know, sweetheart. Mr Mace thinks there will be some improvement and he has built a good eye socket and the implant is in. He seemed quite pleased with that. We can't see a lot at the moment, anyway – it's all bruised and swollen."

"Mum's expecting me to look like I used to. I won't Dad, will I?"

"No, you won't. But it will be better."

I started to cry. Dad passed me a tissue. While I was trying to mop my face – blowing my nose was impossible, it all felt very strange – I heard Dad sniff. That's a shock, when your Dad cries, especially my Dad.

"Dad, I'm sorry, I'm sorry."

Dad took my hand and said the most beautiful thing.

"Cass, I'm sorry. So very, very sorry. I am sorry I wasn't around to protect you and advise you and love you so much that you didn't need to go off in any Tom, Dick or Harry's car. You needed me and I wasn't there. You are my daughter and I should have kept you safe."

I was really crying now. I wanted to tell him it wasn't his fault. That I was old enough to make decisions. That I had made a mistake, not him. That it was part of growing up.

But what I mostly wanted was to turn back the clock. To be a little girl again, to climb on Dad's lap and have a big bear hug. And know I was safe. Does that seem really stupid?

Wish I had your Dad!! Sunday, 27 April 12.43 PM

From: Jennings, Emma [mailto: ejj9@hotmail.co.uk]
To: cassandra briggs
Chapter11.ejj.doc

Wow Cass. If I had to have a big op I would be shrieking the place down. Yelling 'get me out of here' probably. Not being all calm about it, like you.

And I don't think it's stupid to want to feel safe. If I'd ever had a Dad like yours, even I'd want hugs from him.

After your chapter, this one's a bit feeble. It's about school, Miranda, nightmares and seeing your Mum.

See you tomorrow.

Luv

Em x

11

by Em

That week you were having your op, was an ordinary school week for me. I was having the usual ups and downs. The coursework was piling up, because, as you know, I had not been working particularly hard and now all the deadlines had arrived. A bit of me wanted to just coast along and get whatever grades I ended up with. But something had changed for me. I felt that it was really important that I got on with my life because I never knew what was round the corner. Oh yes, and I still felt real guilty 'cause of what happened. Will I ever get rid of that feeling that I should have done something? Maybe it will be there all my life.

Some of school I was enjoying. It helped me take my mind off you. I felt much better about Child Development now that the two projects were out of the way. My Dance GCSE coursework was coming together. The portfolio I had about choreographing my dance wasn't too bad to do. I found heaps about contemporary dance on the Net. Susie suggested that I should draw some of my moves and write about them. She said to call the ones that I'd just made up the 'freestyle' ones and explain them. It was all going ok, 'cept for Miranda. When I tried out some steps, she made some real sarky comments about my dancing.

"Quite the little namby-pamby ballerina on the quiet, aren't you? All that waving your arms about – you look like a windmill. Surely you aren't going to do that on stage?"

I asked Miss Tibbetts if I could go in a different group. I knew she'd say no, and she did:

"Far too late Emma, we are only a few weeks from the final performance. In any case, working in small groups is all about managing to overcome the obstacles of 'conflicting personalities'. Think of this as a wonderful opportunity to get to know Miranda better."

You can guess what I thought of that! Miranda wasn't even interested in showing me her dance. She said she didn't need any practice. Her dance was perfect and anyway, I might pinch her ideas. She wouldn't even tell me which music she was using. But, fair enough, I hadn't chosen mine so she might've thought I'd nick hers.

Polly was the third member of our group. She just did what Miranda suggested most of the time. She had worked out her dance though. She even asked Miss Tibbetts for advice on whether it matched the music she had chosen. That was some jazz – Scott Joplin I think. Oh, you've heard it now, so you know the one I mean. Anyway it's a bit fast so Polly seemed to have trouble fitting all her steps in. When Miranda went to the loo, I suggested to Polly that she simplified the bits where it went a bit random. You know, maybe doing kicks instead of jumps and turns.

"Oh – yes – great, I'll try that. Do you think that I will get marked down, if it's simpler?"

"Probably not. It will fit the style of the music better."

We tried a bit together on the stage. It worked really well and we were both laughing when Miranda came back. She stood and glared at me. Talk about giving me the evils.

Polly went all quiet then, but when she tried her routine again, she was using my ideas. I remember wishing Polly would get away from Miranda. She's cool when she's not with her.

Out of school felt real odd. I went down to Tesco's car park to meet up with everyone. The girls were there – Jackie and them – but the boys never showed. I had half-expected Spider to turn up with some new car. I'd have shopped him if he had. Jackie had brought a can or two. They offered me one, but, you know, I couldn't be bothered with drinking. I chatted for a bit then I went back. I tried to talk to Susie about it, but I couldn't really explain what was wrong.

I was getting some strange nightmares, back then. Real strange. There was you on the grass covered in glass and sometimes you were dead and at other times you went 'Boo' and leapt up, right as rain. But the worse one was when you went over a cliff and I ran after you and we were both falling. When I woke up, Sam was usually crying and Susie was with him telling him I was having bad dreams. So I must have been well shouting. I had to put my headphones on and listen to my music to get off to sleep again. I had it right loud to drown out everything else in my head. It didn't always work.

It must have been about two days after your op that I went and saw your Mum again, Cass. Did I ever tell you about that?

It was just after school. I knew Susie wouldn't be in because she was at a foster carer's day. Learning how to cope with me, I bet!

I really missed you and wanted to see you to have a real good natter. But I had no way of getting to the hospital. Anyway I didn't know how long it would be after your op before you could have visitors. So your mum was like the next best thing, really.

When she answered the door, she didn't really seem pleased to see me. She said something like 'Oh, hello Emma. It's you.' As if she was expecting someone else.

She didn't exactly invite me in, but I followed her through to the kitchen. She put the kettle on. I didn't like to tell her I didn't really want a hot drink. As you know, I only drink tea in an emergency.

"How's Cass, er, Cassandra, Mrs Briggs?"

"She's recovering from her operation, thank you, Emma."

I wanted to ask whether you were pleased with the op. Whether it had done the right thing. You know, all those sort of questions. Instead, I said

"Well, that's really good Mrs Briggs. Does that mean she'll be home soon?"

Your Mum sort of gaped at me. I don't think she'd thought about you coming back home.

"Well, I really don't know, I'm sure."

Your mum busied herself with making us a cup of tea. She makes it a bit strong, doesn't she? No offence – but if I do drink the stuff I like it sort of milky and with lots of sugar.

She put the two cups of tea on the tray. Then just stood there.

"Shall I carry this through for you?" I asked her.

She nodded – so I grabbed the sugar bowl and two teaspoons and put them on the tray before I took it through.

Your mum had gone all quiet again, like she had before when I came. She was sat on the sofa, opposite your picture. It was ages before she said

"Her face won't go straight, you know. It will always be lopsided. And the scarring will have to be covered up."

"She'll be ok, though." I said it. I wasn't sure it was true. I don't know how I'd be, Cass, if my face was damaged like yours. I didn't know how strong you were then – you know, feelings-wise.

"Will she, Emma? Do you think she'll be ok? She wanted to be a singer or a musician. Do you think she'll be able to do that?"

"Maybe she'll have other operations? Maybe she'll have some other treatment? What about these face transplants they're doing now?"

Your mum just shook her head. I didn't know then that you'd discussed all this with Mr Mace and that you had decided that enough was enough for now. I didn't know anything about all the risks of operations and things. Nor anything about face transplants. Mind you, having someone else's face! I'm not sure I could do it. I wouldn't know who I was.

We sat there for a while. I couldn't think what to say. I took her tea from her – it was only half-drunk, but pretty cold I should think. Then I went and washed the mugs up. I was thinking like mad all the time. By the time I went back in your front room, I had remembered something.

"Has Cass seen the psychologist? She's someone to talk to about it all isn't she? She might talk to you about things. You know, like Cass getting back to school and everything."

Your mum just nodded again. I felt really mean, because she'd seemed a bit better when I first came and now she was down again.

"I'd better go, Mrs Briggs. Can you give Cass my love when you see her. And can I visit her at the weekend?"

"I expect so. Yes, I think she wants to see you." She stood up and came with me to the door.

"I thought this operation would make a big difference, but Cass seems more miserable," she said.

I didn't know what to say to that.

"I'll help her however I can," I told your mum, "whatever she has to face."

Trust me to put my foot in it.

Mrs Max Factor Monday, 28 April 8.33 PM

From: cassandra briggs [mailto: cassab88@yahoo.co.uk]
To: Jennings, Emma
Chapter 12.CB.doc

Hi Em

I quite enjoyed writing this bit – it always makes me smile thinking of 'Mrs MF'. I don't know why I didn't realise about Spider then, though.

This happened after the week you've just written about. Must've been the following Saturday.

I had no flashbacks writing this. In fact, it made me feel really positive. Maybe your social worker is right that it helps to get things down on paper.

But, I must resist the temptation to write more. It sort of takes you over, doesn't it? But there's revision, revision and more revision to do (of course!). Exams start in less than three weeks! I don't know why I'm working so hard, no-one expects me to do well in my GCSE's.

I feel really unprepared because I missed the proper mocks.

Give little Sam a big hug from me.

Love

Cass

12

by Cass

On the Saturday, the Max Factor lady arrived. She's a real character, isn't she Em? What was her name? Doreen, I think – but for me she was Mrs Max Factor. She was awesome! She had fitted me in because of my age – she didn't work on a Saturday usually – but she said 'she really felt for me', so made an exception.

Actually, that wasn't exactly a good start.

"I don't need anyone feeling sorry for me." I said.

"Well, that's lucky because I don't. I've just worked with lots of young ladies before and I know how they fret until they see me."

I shrugged, unimpressed. I hadn't fretted at all, because I didn't think anyone could do anything for my face now. I was disappointed after my op. Even though the swelling was going down I could see I was left with a real mess. Where they had put in the bone to make a new eye socket, it had sort of pulled my face across. Probably not too far, but it was already wonky from the scarring so, to me, it looked worse. When Mum had gone home and no-one was around I would look in the mirror and pull my face this way and that to try to make it match the other side. It didn't. And now I had this terrible implant in my face – a blank piece of plastic with no eye on it. At least I could cover that with an eye patch.

Mrs Max Factor was putting bottles and stuff out on one of those little chrome trolleys the nurses use. She was talking away to herself, obviously working through a mental list of things she needed. Then she turned to me

"Office chair. That's another reason why we come on a

Saturday. It's so much easier to borrow one."

She left the room and returned a few minutes later wheeling a squeaky chair. I watched her while she fiddled about until she managed to raise it. She was immaculate! She had long fingernails – which worried me a bit – beautifully manicured. She smelt of Christian Dior or something else expensive, I'm not too good on perfumes. Her skin was really smooth and her eyebrows carefully shaped. She had her dark hair back in a bun-type style, only not dragged back – just gentle. She was probably in her thirties. I wished I'd brushed my hair before she came.

She chatted. Non-stop. All about the make-up she'd once done for some film thing and how that's something she always wanted to do, but somehow she had started doing camouflage make-up for people like me and she 'lo-oved it!!'

"Why?" I asked

"Because we meet normal people. In the film industry the reasons for the make-up are so different. People like yourself, well you're an ordinary girl who wants to look her best. You don't need to look like a person in a period drama, or an old lady. You just want to look like you and feel good about yourself."

By now I was sat on the office chair, which was raised as high as it would go. Because my leg was still needing support, she had borrowed a footstool from somewhere and checked I was comfortable. The chair had quite a high back and plastic arms to it, so I felt all right even though I had only sat up in bed or on that dreadful vinyl armchair in my cubicle before that.

Mrs Max Factor pulled all my hair off my face and put it a big wide hair-band round it. Luckily she left the eye-patch where it was. It would have freaked me out if she had seen that blank implant.

She stood back with her head on one side studying my face. I looked in the mirror she had put on the trolley. Every scar and bump showed. I started to sweat. I felt grotesque. I was hoping desperately that no-one would come visiting. I started to take off the hair-band

"Don't bother, I'm beyond it." I said. She took both my hands in hers and firmly placed them on my lap.

"You'd be surprised what we can do to help you. Just wait and see."

She moved the mirror away as casually as she could. But her doing that made me realise she understood a bit.

Well, you know me, Em. I'm not exactly good with make-up. You are the one who used to put eye-liner on me for parties etc. Although I always did like lipsticks – I had (well, still have) a really good range of those.

She started to explain the various pots and tubes she had in front of her. Everything had to go on both sides of my face to keep the colour and texture even. There was a barrier cream first, to keep my scars from infection, then a foundation base make-up, cover make-up and some sort of top coat to make it all look more natural. I'll show you when you're next round at mine.

She was there all morning, more or less. She tried various colours and various densities of foundation. I got more and more interested as she went along. Every now and again she flicked the mirror up to give me a quick view of the colour she'd put on my lips, or the match of the top-coat. More than an hour after she started, she stood back with her head on one side again.

She picked up the mirror.

"Well, young lady, shall we see what we think?"

I nodded, glumly, expecting the usual lumpy horror with make-up plastered thickly all over it.

She turned the mirror round.

"Have we achieved something here, or have we not?"

Maybe it was because I had expected nothing would work, but to me the change was incredible. Not that I looked like a model or anything, or even like I used to look, but the scars showed less and the make-up didn't look too bad. It made me look well-groomed. It didn't even seem as thick as Miranda usually wears hers. A lot of the redness of the scars had gone, and that made my skin seem a lot smoother. I wanted to smile, but I was frightened I'd spoil the look.

Mrs Max Factor waited for a bit, then said again

"Have we made an improvement?"

"Yers," I said, trying not to move my peach-coloured lips.

She laughed.

"You can talk you know! It won't all crack. Are we pleased with it, or not?"

"I am!" I said. "Very pleased with it."

"Right then," she said "we will borrow a wheelchair and we will go down to the canteen and show you off to the world. Then we'll come back and do it all over again, so that we can teach you."

"No, you go and have a break in the canteen. I'm fine here."

"Sorry, Cassie. It's part of my job. We have to see how the make-up performs in different light – not just under this fluorescent one. We are going to the canteen."

I don't know if I believed her, but we went. I felt really self-conscious and kept pulling my hair over that side of my face. I'm sure people kept looking at me. She had let me put my sunglasses on, to try to hide the eye patch, so I suppose that made me stand out more in the middle of winter. My skin still felt the same, but whenever I touched it, Mrs Max Factor said,

"We said no touching of the artwork, didn't we?"

She parked me over near the window of the canteen and bought me a coke. She took little sips from her black coffee and resumed her chatter. I was hardly listening though. I was just pleased to be doing something off the ward.

When we got back she had just finished showing me how to put it on myself and written out loads of instructions when you knocked on the door. I am so grateful to you, Em – you just came, looked at me and said 'Wow!', then you were laughing and congratulating Mrs Max Factor and then me – because she told you I had done the last application. It felt so good. I know I only looked 'better' and still had a facial disfigurement, but I felt so much more normal.

Then Spider arrived. Mrs Max Factor was packing everything up.

"Ooh is this the boyfriend? I must meet him. And we must have his opinion, mustn't we? Doesn't she look beautiful, haven't we done a good job?"

I felt sorry for Spider then. He obviously didn't think I looked beautiful and he didn't know what to say. He cleared his throat a few times then he did his best:

"See you've got make-up on Cassie babe. That's nice."

"Ooh, don't we despair of men, Cassie. They don't know a good thing when they see it. What do you think Emma?"

"I think he's having a bad day – or needs glasses. Cass looks wonderful. C'mon Cass – if you can go to the canteen with Doreen, then you can with me. Let's have your second outing of the day."

I wasn't sure it would be much of an outing, but I knew I didn't want to be left with Spider.

"Only if you'll let me treat you," I said, "I haven't spent any money for ages."

You grabbed my purse from the table over the bed and we set off.

"I'll leave you girls to it," said Spider. "See you later Cass."

"I don't know where he's going," you said, as he walked off in the opposite direction to us, "that's not even the way to the exit. I must've really offended him."

"Don't worry" I said, "let's buy some chips in the canteen".

Here's a chapter about chips and chocolate

Thursday, 1 May 6.45 PM

From: Jennings, Emma [mailto: ejj9@hotmail.co.uk]
To: cassandra briggs
Chapter13.ejj.doc

Hi Cass
Guess what? I have a sort of date tonight! I'm so excited. But I can't think of anything to wear. I'm only meeting up with Jock and the others for the evening, but J asked me himself and he's calling round to pick me up, so it feels like a date!! Might just be him being friendly, I s'pose.
I read your last chapter – I'm sorry if I scared Spider off. I was hopping mad that he couldn't find anything nice to say. Your face did look heaps better. I thought the change was real dramatic, considering that it was only make-up. Wasn't that Doreen funny? Everything was 'we'. I liked her though. I think she's ok.
This is what happened next . . .
Luv and hugs
Em x

13

by Em

I didn't tell you at the time but Spider rang me later. He said we'd better get our act together and work out when we went to visit you. He said he wasn't very happy being there with me. The cheek of it! I told him in no uncertain terms that I was your friend and that I would visit whenever I wanted, or whenever you wanted. I wasn't going to be bossed around by him.

You know what he did? He used that line he used on you –

"I really like it when you're angry, Em."

I just hung up on him. It is so hard to be nice about him. I hope you understand now why I was always so negative.

We caused a panic that day, though, didn't we? I didn't know we were meant to tell the ward sister, or whatever it is they call her (charge nurse?) if you were going off the ward. It was the first time we'd done it. There were other people waiting for the door to be released. We just followed them out and zoomed along the corridor then down the lift to the café.

You ate, if I remember rightly, 1 all-day breakfast, 1 portion of chips, 1 bath bun, 1 Muller rice, a packet of plain crisps and then you bought a Mars bar (for later). I ate a portion of chips and a Mars bar. We each had a coke. You re-did your lip colour three times, and that was more embarrassing than the amount you were eating! You had just clambered back into your wheelchair when Sister Trendall, arrived.

"Cassandra Briggs. Where do you think you have been? Your mother has been here for 35 minutes and is threatening to make a formal complaint because we couldn't find you."

She completely ignored me and just marched off, pushing the wheelchair towards the lift. I picked up your bag and the Mars bar and hurried to keep up.

When we got back to the ward, your mum was standing by the nurses' station. She was sort of jigging on the spot. You called 'Mum' and she turned round.

"Cassandra. Where on earth have you been? I've been waiting for you! And what have you done to your face?"

"Don't you like it, Mum?"

"Of course I do. Has that make-up person visited you already?"

"Yes, Mum, come and see all the stuff she left me."

Your mum just wheeled you away and Sister Trendall and I were left looking at each other.

"I don't think she'll be making that complaint." I said

"No thanks to you, young lady! It's a really good thing you took Cass to the canteen, but please tell us next time."

"Ok – I'll try to remember."

I was going to come and join you and your mum, but then I thought better of it.

"I'd better go," I said to the ward sister, "could you say goodbye to Cass for me?"

"No problem," she said.

An op or an opt out Sunday, 4 May 3.45 PM

From: cassandra briggs [mailto:cassie88@yahooo.co.uk]
To: Jennings, Emma
Chapter 14.CB.doc

Hi Em
I don't know that you did scare Spider off. I think maybe he was embarrassed about going to the canteen with me. Remember how he was later when we wanted to go out?
I've been having a think about a few things.
I know I keep changing my mind about this, but I might not ever have another op – I keep getting it in my mind that it's for other people not me. You know – to save them being embarrassed about how I look. Should I just concentrate on trying to accept it myself?
What do you think?
Love
Cass
Ps Didn't see you after the Maths revision session – how was your date? One text from you saying 'do wishes come true?' didn't exactly tell me much!

14

by Cass

I had a real low for the next few days. Partly because of Spider, but mostly, I think because I had felt better about myself and then all the doubts set in. The psychologist came on the Wednesday and I spent about an hour with her.

The psychologist, Annette Thomas, turned out to be the lady who had tried to speak to me when I was first becoming aware of what had happened. She is perhaps a bit younger than my mum. She has black longish curly hair and wears trendy clothes and dangly earrings. She was a bit worried about my mood, I think. She did some sort of checklist of all my symptoms. I was getting those bad dreams, well, nightmares. And all the thoughts about the accident.

She had a soft, careful voice. All therapeutic.

"Tell me what those thoughts are like, Cass?"

I had a go –

"Well, it's when I'm trying to do something and there's a little reminder of the accident. Not usually my face, because I avoid looking at that. But things like my revision notes."

"Why revision notes?"

"I had some in my pocket, all folded up, when I had the accident. Mum had straightened them out and put them in the right folder. They sent some work in from school, and so I opened up my folder and they were there. It was horrid. I felt like I was in the car again."

Honestly, Em, it's really strange talking to a psychologist. It's almost like they make you say things you wouldn't tell anyone. I hadn't dared tell Mum in case she thought I was going mental.

"Then what happens?"

"I get all breathless and panicky."

She said it was quite normal. Lots of people get these feelings after an accident – that's when she told me about 'flashbacks'. I felt better knowing that other people had them. That's a bit mean, isn't it?

Then I asked her why I felt so miserable now after feeling a bit better after having my face done. We talked about all my scared feelings of leaving hospital, going home and getting back to school. I felt a bit stupid, though, because whoever feels scared about going home? Annette didn't seem to think like this.

"You will find life difficult for a while, Cassie, because your life has changed and you don't feel like you anymore. Hospital has become a safe place."

"It's awful in hospital, but I know what you mean. The doctors and nurses know how to look after me."

"You wouldn't want to be here forever, though, even it were possible."

I nodded.

"Let's help you feel more in control of the situation. If you were going to learn to swim, how would you do it?"

"I'd have to get in the water . . ." I couldn't think what she was getting at.

"Yes, absolutely! So what is the equivalent small step to getting back home and getting on with your life?"

"Maybe I could try a day home, or even two. As long as I could come back. Would I be able to do that?"

"Certainly – I can recommend a gradual return home to your consultant."

That was the week before Easter – so I spoke to Mum about coming home for part of Easter weekend. She was up at the nurses' station trying to sort it like a shot.

"Sister rang the consultant, and he's more than happy for you to go home that weekend. He said you can go for all three days,

Cassandra."

"No, Mum, two will be plenty." My mum opened her mouth as if to argue with me, but shut it again.

"Maybe it can be three days next time," I said, then added, "Which days is Carl working over Easter, Mum? It might be better if I have some of the time just with you."

You know, even as I said this, I realised Carl hadn't been up to the hospital once. Mum and I just looked at each other. She didn't say anything.

"Don't say it's over." I said – but I was hoping it was.

Mum just nodded.

"How could he leave you at a time like this? That is so unfair!"

"I told him it was finished, Cassandra. I was going against my beliefs. I came to my senses after he asked me to let him move in. He wasn't the man for me."

I don't know whether it's seeing that psychologist, or what. But suddenly I had 'insight'. I realised that I hadn't liked Carl because although he was quite a nice bloke, he was just like another child in our family. You know, always wanting Mum's attention and cross when she spent time with me. But Mum had really liked him.

"I'm sorry Mum."

"Don't be sorry – it wasn't right. Anyway, I'm not really over your Dad yet."

Later, when she'd gone and I was trying to sleep, I started to think about my parents. Why had they split up? I was too realistic to hope they'd ever be back together again – after all Dad was in a new relationship – but they had been good together in a sort of way. They'd been great parents to me. They sort of complemented each other, fitted together. I loved them both even though they were so different. They didn't have to be the same as each other to stay together. Parents can be so stupid.

Short chapter 15 Monday, 5 May 6.45 PM

From: Jennings,Emma [mailto: ejj9@hotmail.co.uk]
To: cassandra briggs
Chapter15.ejj.doc

Hi Cass
Just a short chapter this time. About your first visit home.
Decided date wasn't really a date. It was just the same as other times when we all go out together. I kept wishing it was a date with him, though.
Must go, promised to bath Sam 'cause Susie's got a friend coming round this evening. She's cooking something exotic I think. I don't mind – Sam and I had fish and chips with mushy peas. Then he wanted to go out in the garden to play with the rabbit. It was well muddy, so now Sam is filthy!
C u 2morrow.
Luv and hugs
Em x

Ps forgot to say, I don't think you should have the next op for anyone except yourself. If you don't want it, then don't have it
.

15

by Em

I was so excited you were coming back for the weekend, Cass. I changed all my plans in case you needed me there. Not that I had any really. 'Cept to go with Susie to see if there was anything I could wear to the prom. Just a tour round the charity shops I think. They're that expensive. That could wait. Anyway, she's a wizard with the sewing machine so I knew she could always make me one, if she had time.

It was twelve weeks to the day since the accident. You had missed Christmas, more or less and your Mum said that there would be a 'bit of a celebration, nothing much'. She was baking all week. I went round one evening to help. We cleaned your room and put up the welcome poster and the balloons.

Your Mum was well excited. You'd have thought the Queen was coming. She had washed down walls and shampooed carpets. She'd taken down your big photo-picture thing and put up something else all blue and abstracty that she had bought from John Lewis. It looked well good. I helped her change the furniture around a bit, too, so that you could move about with that walker thing. Then she was worried you wouldn't be able to get up the stairs. So we had a change of plan. We moved the table out of the dining room and put it in the garage and we got a folding bed from the attic and put it up in there. So I cleaned your room for nothing! By the way, I can't believe the amount of stuff your family has up in that attic. All Susie's got is a loft-thing with a ladder that folds down. You can hardly get anything in it.

Anyway, then we decorated the dining room, now bedroom, with those posters and balloons. Because I was there so long, Susie rang to check I hadn't been abducted on the way home.

When I got back I texted Jackie and Polly and a few others. I sort of fell into making all those plans for the weekend. Sorry Cass, I should've asked you first.

Home sweet home Tuesday, 6 May 8.30 PM

From: cassandra briggs [mailto: cassab88@yahoo.co.uk]
To: Jennings, Emma
Chapter 16.CB.doc

Hi Em
I'm sorry, I hadn't appreciated how hard you'd worked. You must've thought I was an ungrateful cow when I came home and wanted to hide away. Here's how things felt for me, so maybe you will be able to understand a bit better.
Bit random, have you noticed it's getting easier to write? Maybe it's because we are improving or it might be that we're writing more recent stuff – most of which is less traumatic. What do you think?
See you in school, Friday.
Love
Cass

16

by Cass

I don't think anyone quite realised what a big thing it was for me to come home. I know it was only for a weekend, but before that all I had done was go to the canteen a few times. I wasn't prepared for the big bad world – even with my make-up on.

When Mum came to fetch me, I was having trouble covering my scars. It had seemed really easy when Mrs Max Factor was there to stop me going wrong – but somehow when I did it on my own it came out blotchy and uneven. Within a week of her showing me, I had taken a great dislike to the whole business. I was getting more and more frustrated at trying to get it right.

In the end my Mum had a go. I could feel her very, very gently touching my skin. Her face was really close to mine and she couldn't disguise the fact that she was slightly wrinkling up her nose as she touched my scars. I sat very still and upright, willing myself to let her do it, then suddenly I had had enough and I pulled away.

"I can't cope with this for next hour or however long it takes – I'd better get on with it myself."

My poor Mum. She didn't know what she'd done. But I had a more successful go at sorting it out when I felt angry – so I suppose in a way she'd helped me.

I moussed my hair and pulled it across my face. I was still wearing the eye-patch, so I tried to hide the elastic amongst my hair. I just wished it would grow faster, my lopsided mouth was sticking out of the bottom of it. I put on my big sunglasses. I felt very nervous.

"Come on Mum. What are we waiting for?"

Sister Trendall insisted that I was wheeled downstairs in the wheelchair, even though I was using the walker thing quite a lot now. My hip was nearly healed, they said, but I must be careful not to put too much weight on it for long periods. So the walker was across my lap. I felt like an old granny.

Getting in the front seat of the car was ok. Travelling in it was not. Of course, the last time I was in a car was when Spider was about to kill us. My head was spinning. I even shouted at my mother to slow down. But worse of all, everyone was looking at me. Everyone.

I've spoken to the psychologist since and she has explained that it always seems like that if we are feeling self-conscious. It's all in the mind, or something. But I started to hide my face. Not just with my hair, but with my cardy.

"For goodness sake, Cassandra, stop drawing attention to yourself. And anyway, I can't see round you with your cardigan up like that."

I started to cry. My mum went very slowly, trying to talk to me at the same time. I had my hand across my face now, and I could feel the oiliness of the make-up on my fingers. I suddenly had the thought that I would never be kissed. No-one would ever cover my face with kisses – they would get all sticky. Anyway, who would want to?

Eventually, we arrived home. I hobbled into the house with the walker, hoping none of the neighbours would see me. I just wanted to hide.

Which is why I didn't cope very well when you, Jock and Spider leapt up from behind the sofa, shouting 'Surprise!' I didn't know what to do with myself. I turned and tried to get up the stairs.

"Not there, Cassandra. Come on, I've made up a bed for you in the dining room." My Mum was gently turning me and manoeuvring me around the furniture. I wanted to scream.

You said something like "We'll come back later." Spider wanted to stay, but Mum said it would be best if he went. He then said

"Well, I'm not sure what I'm doing later. I might see you tomorrow, Cassie babe."

That was the final straw, really. It took Mum ages to calm me down after you had gone.

After lunch – soup – did Mum think I was an invalid? You were back. It was not too bad when it was just you, but we chatted in a sort of polite way as if we didn't know each other very well. It was like being visited in hospital, only I was in my own home.

Then we watched telly for a bit and things felt better. Mum invited you to stay for dinner and made her awesome spag bog. I was just beginning to enjoy being home until you started to plan Sunday for me.

"If you are in the wheelchair, we can do the egg hunt up on the green. I think that's at two o'clock. Jackie will be there and maybe Polly from school."

"I thought you didn't like Polly."

"I'm getting on better with her now. Well, when Miranda's not there as well. They are all really looking forward to seeing you – so are heaps of other people. You're going to be a real celebrity."

"Except I'm not going."

"You've got to go, Cass, everyone's expecting you."

"Then they will have to be disappointed. I'm not going anywhere to be stared at."

"But they're your mates!"

"They didn't visit me in hospital. And anyway, if heaps of people want to see me, then they can't all be my friends. I simply do not have, and never ever have had, heaps of friends."

"But Cass, they couldn't visit you while you were there – your Mum wouldn't let them. I've told them you're home for the weekend. They'll want to see you."

I remembered what the psychologist said about going at my own pace. There was no way I was meeting loads of people. I didn't want to, and maybe I wasn't ready.

"I'll come round tomorrow and see what you want to do," you said.

Do you know? I started to realise then that no-one knew what I felt like – no-one at all, not even you.

You turned up on Sunday at 11 am – I had slept properly for the first time since the accident. I still didn't want to go out, though. Not this first time. My Mum answered the door.

I was just inside the living room and I could hear what was being said. My Mum, bless her, was really firm but polite.

"She really doesn't want to go anywhere, Emma, I'm afraid."

"It's ok, Mrs Briggs, I thought about it when I got home. I was a bit pushy, I think. Would she prefer it if some of us came and visited her?"

"Would you like to ask her yourself?"

You came in with your apologetic face on. It made me smile.

"Sorry," you said.

We had a chat about the day. I didn't mind you coming round, although I didn't want to make you miss the egg hunt. It had been a really good laugh last year – the little ones all went first and 14's to 16's were left really struggling to find any eggs at all. We'd all ended up with quite a few though. Next year we would be too old.

We reached a compromise – you could come after the hunt, as long as you brought me some of your finds – and you could bring Jock and maybe Jackie if she wanted to come. I couldn't face Polly at the moment and didn't see why I should.

It was about five when you arrived. Mum guessed you'd all be hungry and sliced up a huge chocolate cake. Jackie came, complete with a get well card. She handed it over to me with a complete poker face – probably struggling with what I looked like.

"Well, thanks for the thought, Jackie, but actually, I'm not ill!"

"No, but, well. You've been through it, you know. And you are still sort of in hospital."

She didn't say much all the time she was there. We watched a film on TV – something sloppy and romantic – was it Sleepless in Seattle? Then she did a sort of 'oh is that the time, I must rush' and left us. I felt relieved – it was like being on show with her there.

I didn't know if I'd ever be ready to go out and meet everyone from school.

Chapter 17. Meeting up with Mum

Friday, 9 May 6.15 PM

From: Jennings, Emma [mailto: ejj9@hotmail.co.uk]
To: cassandra briggs
Chapter17.ejj.doc

Hi Cass
Thanks for chapter 16. I'm sorry you thought I didn't understand! I did my best to, but you know sometimes I just get it wrong. I really wanted those two days to be special for you.
One thing, it was Notting Hill we watched, not Sleepless in Seattle. We watched S in S some other time. Not that it matters. I've written a bit now about seeing my mum in the Easter holidays, but I don't know if that's really important for getting everything down about the accident. Writing it helped me though.
Time 4 t – better go!
Bye for now. ☺
Luv
Em x

17

by Em

There's usually a visit to see my mum about Easter time. I'd forgotten about it until Susie reminded me. Jen turned up on the Wednesday following Easter Day. As I climbed into her beat-up Renault I felt like a prisoner.

"I don't want to go," I told Jen as calm as I could.

"How much don't you want to go? Just normal nerves, or what?" asked Jen.

"Bit more than nervous. It's such a waste of time. She never knows what to say to me. She's not like my mum any more."

"She's changing, Em. She's trying to get her act together."

"It's too late. I don't feel like she's much to do with me now."

"Well, it's up to you. Do you want to cancel? I can probably get hold of her on her mobile phone."

I thought about it for a bit. Jen would stay with me, because it was supervised contact. So I could leave early if it was too awful. Anyway, how would I feel if I was waiting to see my daughter and she said she didn't want to see me?

"No. I'll see her today and try to tell her."

We were meeting in Cambridge. In the Grafton Centre. When Jen and me arrived, my mum was already there. She was perched up at the counter on a shiny stool in one of those coffee places. You know, the ones with tables outside. Not that they really are out in the open, being in a mall.

She was ordering something as we walked up to her. She was wearing a short skirt and had a ladder in her tights. She had shiny black heels and her hair was straight and in a sort of long bob. She looked much the same as ever from the back. But when she turned round, she smiled what seemed to be a real genuine smile.

"Hello," I said. I couldn't bring myself to call her 'Mum'.

"Hello, Em dear. How's my favourite girl then?" It made me cringe. You know, Cass, I try to be forgiving but I can't really be her favourite, can I? Or she'd have changed long ago and fought to get me back.

I mumbled something. She said,

"I want to buy you some real nice clothes today. What do you think?"

"No thanks. I'm all right for clothes."

Mum shrugged and took her cappuccino from the person serving. There was a moment while we stood behind her and watched her stir in the froth on her coffee. Jen picked up a tray and waited to be served,

"What would you like Cass? A hot chocolate?"

"No, nothing thanks."

At Jen's suggestion we all went and sat at one of the shiny tables. Mum was staring at me. It felt like she had x-ray eyes.

"You've lost weight."

"Have I?" I couldn't think how she'd know if I had. I was wearing two thick jumpers and a pair of boy-fit jeans. Not exactly figure-hugging.

"Yes."

Neither of us could think of anything to say. I noticed she looked a bit neater than usual. Her hair was like mine, long and straight. It looked good. Quite shiny. She still felt like a stranger though.

"Your Uncle Joe sends his love," she said.

"Oh, thanks." I wasn't hundred per cent sure who Uncle Joe was. I didn't like to ask. I tried to remember the family tree Jen had worked out for me a time back. I couldn't think if there was an Uncle Joe on it. Maybe he was her new man. I looked at Jen for help. She leaned forward and said,

"Hope you don't mind me asking, but I can't remember who Joe is."

"My cousin – we live in the same street now I've moved."

"Ah, that's Em's second cousin then?"

"Yeh, but she always called him Uncle Joe."

I couldn't remember. I had that real odd feeling I always get when I find out something about my past. I was wishing I'd cancelled this meeting. I started fiddling with my phone. It felt better than talking to Mum. I sent you a text, actually. But I don't know if you knew where I was at the time.

Jen and Mum were chatting away. I half-listened and found out that Mum was working a couple of days a week.

"I'm just doing cleaning and stuff, at the moment. But I expect I'll get a proper job soon."

"That's good news, isn't it Em?" Jen was trying to include me in the conversation.

I shrugged. It made no difference to me.

"You're being really rude, Em," Mum said. "I've come a long way to see you."

I just looked at her. My so-called mum telling me off in public! What right had she? None.

Jen must've seen my face because she stood up and picked up her coat.

"Let's all look at the shops while we're here, shall we? Where do you both want to go? I know, we'll start with Next."

So we all trailed round the shops for about an hour and a half. Mum wanted to buy me something. In the end I gave in and let her get me some jeans in New Look. While she was paying for them, Jen asked me how long I wanted to stay.

"Could we go now?" I asked.

Mum was all right about it. She'd seen me and she'd bought me something. Now she seemed as relieved as me that it was time to go. I had to put up with being hugged and kissed by her. Then I was free!

You know, Cass, I would really love a proper mother. Perhaps she has changed. If so, I wish I could feel something for her. But there's nothing there any more.

A work of art! Tuesday, 8 May 3.46 PM

From: cassandra briggs [mailto: cassab88@yahoo.co.uk]
To: Jennings, Emma
Chapter 18.CB.doc

Hi Em
Thanks for your chapter. It's ok to write about your mum – after all we agreed to put down our feelings that are causing us major stress. Your time with your mum counts as that. She's going to seem like a stranger when you haven't lived with her for years. It must be really hard for you.
Anyway, here's a chapter about a day that felt really important to me. It was my first appointment to see Mr Keen about my new eye.
Love
Cass xx

18

by Cass

When Mum arrived on the ward at 9 am on the following Tuesday, I think she was surprised I was so upbeat. I was really looking forward to my appointment with Mr Keen. For me, it seemed like a big milestone. I nagged Mum for us to leave the ward early, so we were in his waiting room a full thirty minutes before my appointment. Plenty of time to read all the posters and leaflets about taking care of your prosthetic eye, and different kinds of implants, that sort of thing. Mum didn't want to look at them, but I found them interesting.

Finally, Mr Keen opened his door and helped out an old lady with a walking frame. I peered at her to see if she had an artificial eye, but then I realised I was staring, so I stopped. Mr Keen spotted us

"Cassandra, good to see you. Are you both coming in, or would you like to wait here Mrs Briggs? It's up to you."

Mum had half risen from her seat. She looked dreadfully worried.

"You don't need to come in Mum, if you don't want to. I can manage on my own."

Mum neither stood up, nor sat down. Mr Keen came to her rescue.

"Why don't you just stay where you are for now, Mrs Briggs, and Cassandra and I will call you in when we have something to show you or if we need you."

Mum nodded and sat down again. I walked in through the door Mr Keen was holding open for me, feeling my breathing going a bit fast. I needn't have worried. He was so enthusiastic it was catching!

"Here's what we do Cassandra," he moved closer to me on his office chair. I noticed worn marks on the floor where he must've done this loads of times before. He had a leaflet open in front of me and was talking me through it,

"The first step, here, is to take an impression of your implant. Look, this is what we use." He showed me a soft paste. "It sets to a sort of rubbery consistency, so that we have the exact shape to make your eye."

I nodded – I knew all this from the leaflets I had just looked at in the waiting room.

"O-k," I said slowly, not knowing what was expected from me.

"While the paste is setting," he said, waving his hand in the air, "we begin the creative part! I will paint a copy of your other eye while you are here, to get a superb match."

"I didn't know you did the painting yourself!"

"I told you I would create a masterpiece for you, and that is exactly what I will do."

"So when will I have my eye?" I was feeling excited now.

"You will need another appointment, in three or four weeks. That's when I will check it for comfort and make any minor adjustments if they are needed. I will also show you how to put in the eye"

"Can I take it away the same day?"

"Certainly!"

That meant I could go without my eye-patch, or even sunglasses! I would begin to look more normal.

"I'm looking forward to that," I said.

Then it all became a bit strange. It was as if I wasn't a patient any more, but some sort of artist's model! I had to sit still while he studied my eye and began a tiny painting on a circular shape of what looked like plastic. Although he was probably quite quick, it felt like ages while I was trying not to move. When he finished, he gave me a mirror to show me his work, while I compared it to my good eye. It was awesome!

I couldn't wait to show Mum!

I've written about an assembly I'd rather forget

Friday, 9 May 8.15 PM

From: Jennings, Emma [mailto: ejj9@hotmail.co.uk]
To: cassandra briggs
Chapter19.ejj.doc

Hi Cass
I loved your bit about Mr Keen!
Here's a bit about Mrs Pritchard making a fool of herself!
Here comes trouble, Sam's appeared!
Bye
Luv and hugs ☺
Emx

19

by Em

It was the first Year 11 assembly of the term.

We expected the usual talk from the Head. You know, the same old one about this being the term when we should really work. It was our last chance to up our marks. We would regret it if we didn't, etc etc. But, we had about two sentences from her like that, and then Mrs Pritchard said

"Now I have something I would really like you to attend to."

Which, as you know, is her signal for dropping a bombshell.

"You are all aware of the terrible accident that happened which involved one of our best pupils, Cassandra Briggs."

Everyone shuffled a bit, and I thought I must remember to tell you that she called you a 'best pupil'. Sorry, I forgot to, until now!

"Well, as some of you are aware, Cassandra suffered *a facial disfigurement.*"

She put a lot of emphasis on this. Then she looked round for effect. She had made it sound like something we would all like. It gave me the shivers. Everyone stopped poking each other, whispering and sending texts from inside their pockets. It went totally quiet. They were all waiting for her to carry on.

"She has had an *operation* on her face. She also had a broken hip, which is sufficiently healed for her to be considering a *return to school* within the next week or two. I am preparing you for her return now, because you will need to become used to the fact that she looks *quite different* from, from..." she paused long enough for me to wonder how much more she was going to dig herself into the ground.

". . . how she did. I myself have not yet seen her, but am doing so later today and will prepare a plan for her return."

She shuffled around her papers on the lectern thingy. I don't know if she'd made notes, or what.

"Now when Cassandra comes back she will feel very self-conscious. She has a *visible difference* that may make it difficult for some of you to relate to her. But you must *remember* that Cassandra is still herself, she is still your friend. I suggest that you make a *special effort* to try to include her in things you do."

That made me real mad! It sounded like you were some pathetic creature who needs looking after. I was boiling over.

Old Pritchard finished up with some other bit of news. I wasn't listening anymore. Nor was half the year 11's. They were all whispering to each other. Then we were dismissed.

Miranda squeezed past her friends and came up to me.

"What does she look like then? Is she a real fright?"

I tell you, I nearly clocked her one. But I kept my cool.

"She's doing fine, thank you for asking. I'll tell her you asked after her."

Miranda looked gobsmacked. I turned away from her and headed back to the loos. I felt like screaming 'she's still Cass. She is a real feeling person who doesn't want to be treated any differently.'

I reckon old Pritchard had just made it a million times worse for you.

Visible difference indeed! Saturday, 10 May 3.15 PM

From: cassandra briggs [mailto: cassab88@yahoo.co.uk]
To: Jennings, Emma
Chapter 20.CB.doc
Chapter 21.CB.doc

Hi Em
I hate that phrase, *visible difference.* What on earth does it mean? We are all visibly different and that's how we tell each other apart! Mind you, I hate *facial disfigurement*. The description, as well as having it. Mrs P was well out of order talking about me like that. She wasn't exactly a tonful of tact when she visited! But, I am well impressed. It sounds like you coped with Miranda really well.
Here's chapter 20 and 21 – good things as well as bad!
Now I must stop doing random stuff and force myself to revise some History. You know, strange though it may seem, I used to love History. Before. Now it's a real effort to get my mind round it. I know it's two weeks till the exam, but I have loads to learn.
Love
Cass

20

by Cass

It was just over three weeks since my appointment with Mr Keen and I was dying to see my new eye. I could hardly contain myself when it was the right day.

Mr Keen ushered my mum and me into his room. He asked me to sit by the window. There was a small box on the table – I was sure my eye would be in it.

Mr Keen made a few remarks to my mum about the weather and our journey. Then he came and sat by me.

"Is my eye in the box?" I asked – thinking this was a really odd sentence to be saying.

"Yes – I'll show it to you in a minute. It might not be perfect as yet, so be prepared for me to disappear off and make a few adjustments to it."

I nodded. I noticed my hands were feeling sticky. My heart was pounding hard, too. I sent a quick prayer up and felt a bit calmer.

Mr Keen picked up the box and very slowly opened the lid. There, glistening like a new marble, was the lens that would go over my implant. The painting looked really good.

"You'll need to take your sunglasses off and your eye-patch, for me to be able to fit it."

"Oh yes, of course."

I sat there feeling exposed while he carefully lifted my eyelid and inserted the lens. I couldn't really feel it much until I blinked, then the sensation was different, not uncomfortable.

Mr Keen had a mirror on a stand by him. He turned it so that I could see.

I don't know what I expected, I don't know why I had thought that this one piece of acrylic would make a lot of difference. What I do know is that I was really disappointed.

"Oh." It was all I could say.

"It looks a good match," said Mr Keen, cautiously. "Do you see a problem?"

I gulped.

"I'm sorry, the eye is really good. It's the scarring. I didn't think it would look so bad."

My voice was a bit trembly. I was trying not to cry.

Mum came over behind me and looked into the mirror with me. I could feel her hands firmly placed on my shoulders. She must've been holding her breath because there was a little sigh before she said,

"The eye is lovely, Cassandra. And look, it moves a bit. You can hardly tell which is the good one."

She was right, of course. Mr Keen had done a great job. It was just that my eye still didn't look normal because of the unsightly bumpiness underneath it. I was still staring at it in the mirror when Mum moved to one side and Mr Keen's face came into view behind my reflection.

"Why don't you talk to Mr Mace about that scarring, Cassandra? He may be able to suggest something. I agree it does detract a little from such a beautiful eye."

"Or we could contact Mrs Max Factor again," suggested Mum, "she's taught you a lot about dealing with the other scars."

I tried to sort myself out. After all, it was not Mr Keen's job to work on my face.

"The eye is beautiful, Mr Keen. I really like it. Thank you very much."

"It's my pleasure, Cassandra."

He turned my swivel chair towards the light and studied my two eyes. He asked me to blink a few times and I had to look in all directions. Then he stood back and smiled.

"It doesn't seem to need any adjustments at all. I'll just show you how to put it in and out and clean it, and then you can take it home with you today."

So I did – and you've seen the result!

21

by Cass

It had been my idea to come out of hospital properly – after all, if I was ok to come home for weekends, then I was ok to be home all the time. My walking frame was totally redundant after only a few days.

Going out was a problem. I needed a hairstyle that would hang over the right side of my face a bit better, so one of our first outings was when I went to *A Cut Above* where I have been before. Mum had been in and told Karina, the owner, about my facial injuries, and organised a dry cut so that I could keep my sunglasses and make-up on. Karina opened early for me, so to begin with, it was just her.

She acted a bit too breezy.

"Morning, Cassandra. It's so lovely to see you again. May I take your coat?"

She took my hoody and hung it up. It felt strange when I sat in the chair in front of the mirror. I took my sunglasses off. My make-up had been a bit hurried that morning and I could see where it was a bit caked over the scars, especially under my new eye. I tried to smooth my foundation with my fingers while Karina fetched her trolley of scissors and stuff. I felt terribly exposed under those fluorescent lights.

She was behind me now, lifting my hair and studying it. The ends were dreadful – it hadn't been cut since before the crash.

"How would you like it?"

"Umm, like that singer, you know the one, Gabrielle? She used to wear her hair across one side of her face completely covering it."

"But you won't be able to see, dear."

Mum hadn't prepared Karina as well as I had hoped. I found myself stuttering,

"Er, that, um, doesn't really matter. As long as my left eye shows. The other one, um, isn't functional."

"What? It don't work no more? Oh, I'm sorry. I didn't know."

She made a face in the mirror – maybe sympathy, maybe an apology. I shrugged as if it didn't matter. In a way it was good, because she had thought my false eye was a working one! Mr Keen would've been pleased.

Karina started to comb my hair across my face.

"Look, dear, if we part your hair here, like this, then sweep this side forward, then that will do quite a good job of having it like you want, but stylish. It will merge your fringe in too, that's not really quite long enough yet. You might want to straighten your hair with this style, though, because that's the best way of keeping it in place."

So much for an easy style to shake and go!

"I've got straight hair already, so I haven't done that before"

"Yes, well, I give you it's not curly. But it doesn't hang quite the same as straightened hair. Tell you what, I'll cut it, then if you don't mind, I'll just spray it damp and use the straighteners on it and you'll see what I mean."

I nodded. It couldn't make me look any worse than I did now. A bit of me wanted to say 'Oh, cut it all off, who cares?' but I didn't feel quite ready to face the world yet. For the time being, I'd just try to hide it so that I could merge in with everyone. I knew I'd still stand out as the only one in school with a haircut covering one side of my face. That's if it did cover it – I just hoped she didn't make it too short.

"Don't cut too much off, will you?" I said.

Well, you saw the result. It was great – she did a real Gabrielle hairstyle and showed me how to do it at home. The straightening only took her about 10 minutes and seeing as how it took me forty to do my make-up, I didn't think that was too much of an extra job. The other staff arrived while my hair was being done, but they didn't take too much notice. I expect they'd been warned I was coming.

Which is a long way round of telling you that I hadn't been out much! So when Mrs Pritchard arrived in the early afternoon, I was feeling like hiding. Mum let her in – I was waiting in the living room. I could hear they were having a conference about me in the hall – but Mum had closed the door, so I wasn't quite sure what they were saying. Mum led Mrs Pritchard in and she sat on the armchair opposite me.

"Cassandra, it is *so* good to see you."

"Thank you for coming, Mrs Pritchard."

I was trying to read her expression, watching her to see when she would react to my appearance. She didn't. She had a dead-straight poker face – as my Dad would say. But she had no idea how I felt about things, either.

"I have told Year 11 that you will be returning to us very soon."

I didn't know what to say – I'd have rather sneaked back into school than have everyone expecting me. Mrs Pritchard continued

"Your mother seems to think you may prefer to be home tutored, though."

That explained the quiet conversation in the hall.

"We have discussed it, yes. But I don't know what's best."

"Well I do. The sooner you are back with all your friends, the better. And you have a lot of catching up to do."

Catching up for what? I had been all ready to get good GCSE's, do music, English and history at A level and then off to music college to be a performer. Suddenly it all seemed futile.

"I was thinking I might not do my exams."

"Why not? You're a bright girl Cassandra. You are perfectly capable of achieving academically. You will soon catch up."

I tried again,

"I was thinking I might leave coming back until after half-term."

"Oh no, Cassandra, oh no. If you like, we can gradually re-introduce you to school, but you're not really *disabled* so I'm sure you can cope."

My mother was wriggling in her seat, obviously itching to say something. I hated the way Mrs Pritchard was expressing it, but in a way she was right. I was perfectly able to go to school, it's just that, well you know, what would everyone think about my face?

"Cassandra will need to make up her own mind about when she's ready," said my mother.

"Don't worry Mum. I expect it will be all right." I turned to Mrs Pritchard, feeling a little more in control again.

"I know I am not disabled, but life is more difficult for me now and I haven't been to school for nearly four months. If it is all right with you, I would like a gradual re-introduction, just going to the classes where I know I will have Emma Jennings there, at first. Oh, and maybe try a music lesson."

"Well I'm glad you are going to try to come back to school, Cassandra. But you must not build a dependency on Emma. She is a very different young lady to you. I'm surprised there are any lessons in which you are in the same group."

My mother stood up for you, then Em.

"Emma Jennings has been a great help to us both. There is more to her than meets the eye."

I did a mental thumbs-up to Mum.

"Actually, Mrs Pritchard, we are in the same group for Child Development and Theatre Studies. And we both picked optional RE – we are in the same class although we are in different bands for the exam."

"What about the sciences, maths and English, Cassandra? It is extremely important that you do not neglect these core subjects."

"I've been doing a lot of revision in hospital, Mrs Pritchard. And I even sent some test papers in to be marked."

Mrs Pritchard obviously didn't know that. She sort of gave in.

"I'll check with the teachers that you are on course for good marks in those exams, then. If you are, you can have your choice of subjects."

"Thank you."

"We will start with – let me see, Child Development, Theatre Studies, RE and Music. But I would like to review it every week and build you up to the full curriculum as soon as possible."

After she had gone I worried about Theatre Studies. Mr Lang was inclined to pick on us and make us stand up and do things. My mother was all for ringing up and telling him to let me just be at the back for a bit, but I wouldn't let her.

So this brings us to the day I came back, which was only a few days after Mrs Pritchard had spoken to you all in assembly.

I was up at about 6 am! Incredibly early. Mum was still asleep but I was determined to get my face right and straighten my hair. I had a shower, then it took a good hour just to do the make-up, because I kept wiping it off and having another go. I hadn't even asked if I could wear make-up so I was really worried I would be told to take it off. A bit like Estelle in year one, who came with her eczema cream all over her face? Her mum went ballistic when she was sent home. As soon as I heard Mum go downstairs to make a cup of tea, I went and bullied her into writing a note, just in case. She didn't know what to write so in the end we settled on:

> "Dear Tutors,
> Please excuse the use of make-up by my daughter Cassandra.
> This is medically prescribed to cover facial scarring.
> Yours sincerely
> Marian Briggs."

This led to a long discussion about other notes I would need.

Perhaps one to tell them I must sit at the right of the room, because I couldn't see out of my right eye. Or one to excuse my hair being over my face, or permission to wear sunglasses. I still wanted those because of the scarring under my eye. Mum re-wrote the note adding in that I needed to wear sunglasses at this stage of my treatment.

By then I was feeling really nervous. She couldn't persuade me to eat any breakfast. It was still only 7.30 am and we didn't need to leave for a whole two hours, for me to arrive just before period two for Child Development.

"Have a singing practice then while you wait," Mum suggested.

You know, Em, up until then I hadn't done any serious singing at all. I'd sung along to my MP3 player, but with the earphones in. I hadn't really listened to myself.

I got out my GCSE performance piece. I felt like I was stepping back in time – it all seemed so unfamiliar, as if it were blocked out of my mind. I stood by the piano like I always used to and tried limbering up with a few scales – how long was it since I'd had a singing lesson? Months. My voice was croaky, I couldn't reach the notes. I regretted saying I would go back to music – what would I do while the others were getting ready for their performances? There was no way I'd be able to do mine.

So as you can see, I was well wobbled by the time it came to go into school. I wished I'd said I'd go in at the same time as everyone else so that you would call for me.

More writing Monday, 12 May 6.37 PM

From: Jennings, Emma [mailto: ejj9@hotmail.co.uk]
To: cassandra briggs
Chapter22.ejj.doc

Hi Cass
Sounds like you stuck up to Old Pritchard. Fancy her saying we are different kinds of girls. That's so out of order. I know I don't talk all posh like you, but that's discrimination, that is.
But I'm not going to think about her. Here's the bit about you coming back. I was so excited. You've no idea how much I missed you in school. It was awful without you.
brb
Sam was going through my stuff. He's a bit lively tonight so I'd better get him out of my room. Otherwise he'll only break something!
Luv and hugs
Emx

22

by Em

I arrived in the entrance lobby at 9.55 am. On time for once! You were already there, looking out the window. Your Mum was busy talking to someone at reception. I think she was trying to find out where I was, but she needn't have worried. I wouldn't let you down.

"Hi Cass. You ready?"

You turned round and I saw your hair. I thought it was awesome! It was all smooth and bouncy and shiny. Wish I had hair like that. You were wearing those really dark Pierre Cardin shades and you looked well classy. You could hardly see your scars or your eye at all. But you were trembling.

"I don't know if I can do this, Em."

You turned back to look out of the window again and I came and stood by you.

"It's ok, Cass. It will be all right. If anyone is mean to you I'll, I'll clock them one."

You sort of smiled, a bit.

"Come on, Cass. You just give it your best. If it doesn't work out, then at least you'll know you gave it a go."

There was a tear creeping out from under your sunglasses. I grabbed a sort of clean tissue from my pocket.

"Don't mess up the make-up or we'll have to spend all lesson in the loos and I'm getting my project mark today!"

You snivelled a bit, mopped under the shades with the tissue and sort of shook yourself.

"Better go then," you said.

I shouted 'hello and goodbye' to your Mum and tried to keep up with you as we went down the corridor. I just stopped you going into French by mistake. We'd changed classrooms because they needed the video equipment. Then we reached the right room.

I peered through the glass in the door. Yes, we were first, as planned. I'd had to leave maths early (shame!!) because Mrs Pritchard thought it would be best to go into an empty classroom. We found a seat that would be best for you. It was far over to the right and near the front so that people couldn't turn round to gawp at you. I felt strange so far forward. I always worry about what's going on behind me.

Some people didn't even notice you were there at first. They tumbled into the classroom chattering loudly. Jackie said something like "All right, Cass?" sort of quiet-ish as she went past. One or two others just looked. We only have three boys in Child Development. Mickey is the only one who wants to work with children, I should think. But Kevin and Alan just muck around and want to be with the girls. They came in last, those three, and Mickey just stared. I thought he was being real rude until he yelled out

"Hey everyone, Cass is back. Three cheers for Cass!"

Then the whole class started cheering and lots of people yelled "All right Cass?", "How goes it, Cass?" or "Missed you". You remember, stuff like that. You were bent over your books, but your neck went all red and I could see you smiling under all that hair.

"Thanks guys," you mumbled.

Then Miss came in.

"Very good to see you back with us Cassandra." Then, to the whole class, "Shall we all start with a short review of what you remember from last week?"

And that was it. You were back at school and I was well chuffed.

Not belonging Wednesday, 14 May 7.46 PM

From: cassandra briggs [mailto: cassab88@yahoo.co.uk]
To: Jennings, Emma
Chapter 23.CB.doc

Hi Em

You know, it was really strange for me, coming back to school. I didn't feel like me any more – well, you'll see when you read this. It seems a long time ago now, but of course it's only a few months. I still don't feel like the old me. I never will again, I suppose. Sorry – I didn't mean to sound miserable and whiney! It wasn't all bad as you'll see.

Random change of subject – how's your great romance going? Don't tell me there isn't one – I can see there is.

This chapter is about those early days at school from my point of view.

Love

Cass

23

by Cass

You were pleased – yes – but I was finding it really difficult. School had become a major struggle for the first time in my life. I'd been back about three days (part days, to be exact) when I had my first music lesson. I wasn't looking forward to it one bit. In fact, I was very worried. Before school I had felt really sick. But Mum was certain I should go,

"Come on, Cass. Music is your favourite subject. And it's the only lesson you have today, so you'll be home again in next to no time!"

"But I can't sing anymore!"

"Music isn't just about singing, Cassandra. You know that. If your voice isn't up to much, Miss Jenkins will let you play one of your instruments."

"Well, maybe I could try something on the keyboard."

"Of course you could. Now come on."

She bundled me towards the car and I did my usual head down bit so that the neighbours wouldn't see me. I hadn't spoken to either next door at that stage and I didn't want to.

You weren't there to meet me, of course, because you don't do music. I really missed you. Not that I was dependent on you as Mrs Pritchard had suggested – but it just helped to talk to someone while I walked through the corridors. But that day I was on my own.

It seemed like miles through the school and then out the back to the music block. As I approached, I could hear there were people in there already. Someone was banging away on the drums and there was a different sort of tune being played on the keyboard. I stood there for a moment holding the handle, then I took a deep breath, said a quick mental prayer, checked my hair was hanging over my face and walked in.

Everything looked the same – but yet was completely different. The drummer (Mark) and keyboard player (Lyndsay) both suddenly synchronised as they stopped together. Five pairs of eyes were turned to me.

"Hi" I said.

"Hi!" they chorused.

Then silence. It seemed an age before Mark resumed his drumming. Lyndsay was having trouble turning away from staring at my face. I remembered the psychologist's advice about how to deal with those who stare. It took all my effort but I managed it.

"It's scarring, from the crash, Lyndsay. I'm wearing make-up to disguise what I can, but the shape of my mouth is different and so is my eye of course."

"Oh, ok. That's why you're wearing the glasses, is it?"

"Yes."

"You look like that singer with your hair like that. You could make a career as a look-alike."

"I don't think she had scars."

"Oh, maybe not. She wore an eye-patch, didn't she? As a fashion statement?"

"I don't know, did she?"

It was really easy after that. Lyndsay and I just chatted about various stars and then about the piece she was playing for her performance and I told her about my problems with my voice. Then Polly came in and sat with us and she said she liked my new hairstyle. I felt more one of the group than ever before.

Miss Jenkins was late, which was not unusual.

"Cassandra – you're back. I am pleased. We have missed your wonderful voice. Let's start with your piece because the rest are nearly ready for the concert and you will have some catching up to do."

I stood there, wanting to be anywhere else. I could feel the heat rising up through my body into my face. I knew I no longer had a wonderful voice.

"I'm not sure I will be in the concert, Miss Jenkins. Well, not singing."

Miss Jenkins came right up to me and whispered – only more like a stage whisper,

"Cassandra, was your voice . . . damaged?"

"No, well, yes. I don't know. But my voice is all croaky."

"Is that all? Well, what a relief." Miss Jenkins did one of her little twirls – you know what I mean. "Well, in that case, I will give you some exercises and a few tips and we'll soon have you singing like a skylark."

She disappeared into the stock cupboard and the class pretty well forgot about her for a bit and doodled on their instruments. After a while, I looked into the stock cupboard.

"Miss Jenkins, I don't think I can do it. I am very unsure about the concert."

"Found it!" She said, pulling down a folder from the top shelf.

"In this folder, my dear, there is a booklet full of good advice for laryngitis. Now, I know that's not quite your problem but I didn't sing for a whole six months because . . . well never mind why . . . and my voice was terrible! So my singing teacher gave me this booklet and within three weeks I had my voice back."

I just wished I could catch her enthusiasm. I had no expectations that I'd be able to sing again, ever.

The rest of the lesson was mostly revision, although Miss Jenkins did want to hear Polly play her piece. It was a little too advanced for her, I thought, but Polly stumbled through it. I started to think about pieces I could play.

Mum was waiting outside at the end of the lesson. I was feeling so miserable by then that I didn't even feel annoyed at being picked up from school as if I were in the nursery. I had read Miss Jenkins' booklet and found nothing in there that looked like a miracle cure. There was something about steaming your voice – but we didn't even have the special little cup you needed for that. I didn't even mention it to Mum. In fact, I don't think I said anything in the car.

I went straight to my room when I got home. Another disaster day at school. I'd been back only a few days and already things were going wrong.

About an hour later, Mum knocked on the door.

"Come on Cassandra, talk to me about it."

For once I did. I told her about Miss Jenkins and her insistence that I'd be all right for the performance. About how I was certain I would make a mess of it because my voice was rubbish and how I was horrified at the thought of having to go on a stage in front of an audience anyway.

Mum just hugged me like I was some little kid.

"It's ok. You don't have to. I'll write you a note. And if it's not sorted out, you can always leave."

"I'll have to go to school."

"No you won't, I'll tutor you at home!"

Oh, that again. I thought it was an awful idea last time she mentioned it. What did my mum know about Physics, or Maths? She might be able to help with English or Child Development but that would be it.

I could just stay indoors, though. No-one need see me.

Just for that moment, it felt like it might make sense.

Chapter 24: dreadful Monday! Wednesday, 14 May 7.35 PM

From: cassandra briggs [mailto: cassab88@yahoo.co.uk]
To: Jennings, Emma
Chapter 24.CB.doc

Hi Em
Just got time to send this to you before Mum comes back. I was trying to do revision but I kept remembering about this awful day at school, so here it is to get it out of my system.
Fancy asking me in front of Jock today what I meant about a 'romance'. It's him! I'm sure he really likes you! He gets this dreamy look when he's watching you and you aren't looking at him! And he never talks to anyone else when you are around. Honestly, I can't believe you haven't realised.
Back to revision – c u tomorrow.
Love
Cass

24

by Cass

It was the Monday of the third week I was back at school. I was in Chemistry, it was my first lesson without you, so I sat with Big Sue. That new girl, Debbie, was sitting with Miranda, Polly and Chrissie at the back and just before Mr Jackson came in, I could hear Debbie asking Miranda all about me. Miranda didn't even bother to whisper.

"Scarface, you mean! Oh, she's just some little nobody who decided to step out of her league and ended up the worse for wear!"

"What happened?"

"She went for a ride with some boy. She must have distracted him 'cause he crashed the car. It's a write-off – so's she, if you ask me."

They then started whispering and giggling. I just wanted to hide my face but Sue was really angry. I think she'd have hit Miranda, if I hadn't made her sit down.

"Leave them Sue – you'll only end up in trouble. I don't want any fuss."

Mr Jackson had arrived while this was going on. Most of the class went quiet, but Miranda and her cronies were still stirring it at the back. Mr Jackson crossed his arms and just waited. I felt the heat rise in my face as snatches of conversation reached me.

"Blood everywhere . . ." "She just looked moody before. . ."

"That's not a real eye, you know . . ."

Mr Jackson's voice boomed through the classroom

"Is this your Chemistry project you are discussing ladies? Or is it some poison you are concocting? No tittle-tattle allowed in my lesson – any more of it and you will all three have detention."

Miranda just smirked. Debbie muttered "Sorry, Sir" and gave me a bit of a smile as she got out her books. That didn't help – I hated people feeling sorry for me. I just pulled my hair further across my face.

The day got worse. I don't know if I ever told you about what happened in the next lesson. I had Home Economics and it was cooking. For some reason, we had a supply teacher. Can't remember her name, if I ever knew it. The first thing she said to me was,

"Tie your hair back girl – you surely know that hygiene is the first rule of cooking."

I just froze. Someone else said,

"She's excused, Miss. On account of her face."

Then that awful woman came right up to me and lifted my hair and my sunglasses. I could see her swallow before she dropped my hair back and handed me the glasses.

"Well, do <u>not</u> lean over the food. In fact, you had better be the one who clears away and washes up for your group."

If you'd been there, you'd have lost it with her, I'm sure of that. But you know what I'm like – I was mortified. I was trembling and I felt sort of – I don't know – *raped.* She had no right to expose my face like that and just stare at it. Up until that day, I had coped, more or less. I started thinking again that Mum's idea of home schooling wasn't as stupid as I had thought it was.

Sue came to the rescue. As soon as we got into our groups, she gathered me up, almost literally, and gave me one of her great bear hugs.

"Take no notice of that ignorant moo, Cass. She can't watch all the groups at once – you help me cook and I'll help you clear."

So there I was, surreptitiously rolling pastry, and stealthily spooning stewed apple as if I were some thief picking pockets! Sue made it into quite a game and was really pleased when she got 9/10 for her apple pie. What's more, when Miss Tansbury came back next lesson, Sue told her I made the pie and should be credited with it for my GCSE. She's a real softie for a girl who likes playing rugby!

I thought that was enough for the day really – but Miranda wasn't happy with me – probably because of Mr Jackson's scathing remarks earlier. My next encounter with her was at the end of the school day, when I went into the loos.

I could hear Miranda's voice as I opened the door. There she was, with Polly and Chrissie as usual, all three peering into the mirror as she pulled at her chin.

'Oooh, it's huge. It's so AWFUL – I feel like a right ugly freak.'

Chrissie turned and saw me. She nudged Miranda whose steely-grey eyes met my good one in the mirror. For a split second we held each other's gaze, then she turned and announced dramatically:

'Well, perhaps not <u>that</u> much of a freak!'

Polly shrieked a high-pitched, shocked giggle. Chrissie had the decency to go scarlet. I shrugged, turned into the cubicle, then leaned against the graffiti on the closed door. I was clenching my fists tight, struggling not to cry. I managed to hang on until someone flushed a loo – so my sobs were drowned in the sound of gushing water.

I didn't know what to do. I certainly didn't want to push past Miranda to wash my hands. Anyway, there seemed to be some mutiny going on outside – Polly was angry with Miranda. I couldn't believe it – she usually followed her leader.

"There are limits you know. You are well out of order and I am absolutely completely and totally fed up with it."

Miranda's reply sounded almost pleading.

"You found it funny, didn't you? You were laughing."

"I did – but only because you took me off-guard. It wasn't at her, it was you. You are laughable! I've had enough of your bitch-iness. I'm going."

I heard the door slam. Then Miranda's voice,

"Oh, come on Chrissie. We'll go to Macdonald's on our own. We don't need the likes of her around."

You know, Em, she sounded really hurt. I almost felt sorry for her. I marched out of the cubicle without waiting for them to leave and gave them both a big (although rather lopsided) smile.

But I avoided looking in the mirror.

Dancing and stuff Thursday, 15 May 12.38 AM

From: Jennings, Emma [mailto: ejj9@hotmail.co.uk]
To: cassandra briggs
Chapter25.ejj.doc

Hi Cass

Found your email when just about to go to bed. Read your chapter. Did Mrs Pritchard forget about the slow introduction back to school? If I'd been there, I'd have sorted Miranda. She needs her head examined!

Reading your stuff made me remember you helping me find that music. So then I had to write about it! So now it's 12.30 am!!!!! And I'm cream crackered!

Good luck with your music listening exam or whatever they call it tomorrow. Glad I haven't got an exam 'cause I'd have to pin my eyelids to my eyebrows. Or smuggle in black coffee to keep awake.

Luv and hugs

Em x

Ps Do you really think Jock fancies me? I'm not so sure. I thought it was you he liked. No-one ever likes me. Well, no boy. Do I scare them off?

25

by Em

Your awful Monday must have been the same night that I came round to yours 'cause of my dance performance. I'd got an idea for a few steps, and I'd worked out a bit of a routine. But I didn't have music. And you know me, about as musical as a howling dog.

Your Mum answered the door to me.

"Oh, excuse me Mrs Briggs, but could I have a word with Cass?"

"I'm not sure. She's up in her room – she might have gone to bed. I'll go and see."

I remember looking at my watch and thinking 'no-one goes to bed at 7.30.' But your Mum came downstairs and said

"Yes, she's turned in for the night."

I guessed that a) you weren't in bed and b) you were listening. So I spoke nice and loud,

"Oh dear, is she ill?"

"Well no, not really. It's just that she's had a very bad day," said your Mum, just as loud.

"Oh no! I am sorry about that. But I really need her help."

"What for?" This was getting silly. Your mum and me were shouting at each other in the hall.

"It's my performance for my GCSE. I haven't got any music and I thought Cass could help me choose some. Oh no. What am I going to do? I don't know anything about music, I'm real stuck now."

Your voice floated down from above, where you were leaning over the banisters.

"Ok, Em. If it's an emergency, you'd best come on up."

Your mum gave me a little pleased grin.

You didn't tell me all that about Miranda. You did say about that stupid teacher who pulled your hair back. You'd have thought she'd have been told you were in the class, or something. You were really down. I think you were pleased to see me though, really. Weren't you?

It took us a while to put the world to rights as much as we could. You were furious with yourself for not leaving the room to go and find the year head. Or anyone else who could sort things out. Then again, you weren't sure that was the answer 'cause it felt like running to Mummy! But we both agreed that big Sue was a good'un. Even if she did play hockey for the county as well as rugby.

Your mum knocked on your bedroom door.

"Would either of you like a drink?"

You and me exchanged glances. I managed not to be cheeky and ask for a lager! We both had hot chocolate and chocolate biscuits. Then we remembered why I had come and you ran downstairs and came up with loads of CD's. I have never ever listened to so much classical music in one night!

But when you put that Bolero thing on, I remembered those ice skaters. You know, Torville and Dean. There'd been a documentary about them and they showed them winning something ages ago. They skated to that and it was well cool.

"That's the one!" I said.

So we toasted each other by clinking our cups of rather cold hot chocolate and danced around your bedroom to the CD.

Oh yes he does!! Friday, 16 May 10.51 PM

From: cassandra briggs [mailto: cassab88@yahoo.co.uk]
To: Jennings, Emma
Chapter 26.CB.doc
Chapter 27.CB.doc

Hi Em
He so-o fancies you! He never talks to me, not really. Except to ask where you are!
Anyway here's my next bit, from when you came to the door. I've actually done two chapters, 26 and 27. There's a lot about Spider in the first chapter. Sorry about that – I know he's not your favourite subject. But the other one is more about Rob. Bit different, those two, don't you reckon?
Time to grab a bit of sleep – hopefully without nightmares. They are definitely less vivid now – what about yours?
Love Cass

26

by Cass

It was a good thing you came round – sort of. You're right – I was feeling really down. I felt done in from all the effort of trying to just be me. And who was I anyway? I'd forgotten. The present me was who I was struggling to be.

I hid under the covers when I heard someone at the door. I was in no mood to be disturbed. I was in bed with my clothes on – bed felt, I don't know, safe I suppose.

You had your exaggerated voice on – the one you use in school when you are making sure the whole class hears when you are trying to get Miranda off your case. I could have ignored that, but when I heard my mum doing it too I started to listen. I didn't think you'd be asking for help if you didn't need it, so that's when I caved in and got out of bed, took the couple of steps across the landing and called you up.

It did cheer me up to find music for you, and I loved the way you danced. I wanted to do dancing years ago when I was quite little – but I also wanted to play an instrument and someone gave Mum a half-size violin for me to try and I sort of became intoxicated with that and started nagging Mum until I had lessons.

After you'd gone, I went downstairs and made myself some toast and came and chatted to Mum. The doorbell went (again!) at about 9.30. It was Spider! Not exactly the time to come round. I heard him speak to Mum

"I just called round to see how Cassie was, Mrs Briggs. I meant to come earlier but I got delayed."

"You'd better come in." My mum did not sound pleased to see him.

I was mortified. I was sat there with no make-up on and in my old tracky bottoms and no shoes. My hair was all over the place. I tried to pull it straight over the right side of my face while he came into the room.

"Hi Cassie, babe, how you doing?"

My mum muttered something about seeing what was on the telly upstairs and left us.

He came over and flopped down on the settee beside me, throwing his arm round me. I immediately knew why he'd been 'delayed'. He stank of beer. To avoid becoming drunk in the fumes, I stood up.

"Do you want a coffee, or something, Spider?"

He just stared at me. Then he answered.

"Yeah, babe, black coffee. And put some make-up on while you're doing it, eh?"

It was my turn to stare.

"Just joking, Babe, just joking. You know, I ain't seen your face like that for a while. You look a bit strange. That's all."

"I think you'd better go, Spider. Come round earlier next time when I'm still looking . . . a bit less strange."

"Ok, Babe. No offence. Me mates are waiting anyway."

He just couldn't wait to get out of the house.

So that was the reason why I felt so awful next day at school. I couldn't get Spider out of my mind. I found you in the hall at lunchtime, where you had the CD on and were working out a few moves. Some of the rest of the dance performance class were there. Polly was stood by the stage giving you more ideas for steps. The others were standing chatting in a group, two of them I knew from English. Maybe I looked moody and miserable, I don't know, but when I said 'Hi' to them they just said 'Hi' back and then carried on chatting to each other. Then they walked across to sit on the chairs at the other side of the hall. I tried smiling at them as they walked in front of me, hoping they would ask me to sit with them. They all pretended not to see.

I sat on my own, watching you and dying to talk to you about

Spider. I could feel my head beginning to throb and I felt sick. I decided I couldn't wait for you to finish. As I left the hall, Miss Jenkins was walking past. I must have looked how I felt because she asked me if I was feeling all right. When I told her I felt dreadful, she took control.

"Well young lady, you are in no fit state for this afternoon's music lesson. I'm sending you home sick. I will make sure your tutor knows. Off you go."

I took the 1.30 bus and arrived home just before two. I let myself in and was surprised to hear voices in the kitchen. It was Spider! He was laughing with my Mum. They both stopped and looked at me when I came in.

"Hi Babe – I came back at a decent time of the day, like you said!"

I felt too rotten to sort it all out in my mind.

"Yes, well, I've come home sick – sorry, I've got to lie down."

"I'll come up with you to keep you company."

I was pleased, for once, that Mum can be super protective

"I don't think that's a good idea, Stephen. Why doesn't Cassandra give you a ring when she feels better?"

"Bye, Spider," I said. I wasn't sure I wanted to ever see him again.

27

by Cass

I can't remember what happened over the next couple of days, except it was a real effort to get to school. On the Friday, I had an individual lesson arranged with Miss Jenkins. I was absolutely determined to tell her that no way was I singing anything, and that I wanted to be assessed on coursework alone and would work really hard to get any outstanding work in on time.

I waited in the Music Room. It was empty and I walked around doodling on the instruments. Just touching the instruments and playing a few notes helped me relax a bit. Miss Jenkins wasn't due for another five minutes – so she probably wouldn't arrive for another ten. I picked up one of the ropey old school guitars and sat on the edge of a table. I strummed a D chord – it was dreadfully out of tune. It didn't take long to tune it, and I played a little bit of Rodrigo, before starting to strum a song. 'She loves me Yeah, Yeah, Yeah' My croaky voice suited the brash guitar chords. I moved onto other Beatles songs – fiddling around until I discovered the chord sequences. I was singing a passable attempt at 'Strawberry Fields' with mostly the right chords, when a voice behind me said

"I thought you had no voice." She made me jump, sneaking up like that!

"I haven't Miss Jenkins. I can only sing this sort of thing. I can't very well do that for the concert."

"Well, for one thing you could, but it won't match your portfolio, which is definitely A* standard. For another thing, if you can sing like that now, you will certainly be able to sing your prepared piece in three weeks' time."

I had my hand in my trouser pocket – I could feel Mum's note.

I hadn't intended to use it, I was sure I would be able to persuade Miss Jenkins that I couldn't do the concert. I should have sat and waited without picking up that guitar.

"Would I be able to be assessed on my coursework alone?"

"Oh no, I wouldn't entertain the idea. There is absolutely no reason why you shouldn't be able to sing. I'll just fetch the piano score."

She disappeared out of the room and I was left alone again. I pulled the note out of my pocket. I hadn't read Mum's final version – it was nearly open. I pulled out the page filled with Mum's neatest writing.

"Dear Miss Jenkins

As you know, Cassandra has gone through a great trauma that has left her very fragile. She feels unable to sing and, indeed, her voice is not what it was. She is unable to stand up in front of an audience because of her embarrassment about her appearance. Therefore, I am writing to ask you to contact the examination board and request that she should be excused her performance because she is now a child with special needs.

I am sure the assessors will be willing to give her a grade on her coursework alone.

Yours sincerely

Marian Briggs

(Mother)"

I couldn't believe it! My own mother was calling me 'special needs'. And a child, too. I was nearly 16! How dare she?

I screwed up the note and threw it in the wastepaper bin. This was one battle I was going to fight without the backing of my mother.

Luckily Miss Jenkins was ages, so I had a chance to calm down a bit and think. She was hardly back in the room when I asked;

"Couldn't I play the keyboard instead, Miss Jenkins? I have

reached grade 6, so I am sure I could find something to play." I didn't add, 'with my back to the audience' although I was imagining that.

"Look, Cassandra, you have a beautiful voice and I want to hear you sing in that concert. Obviously I can't make you sing, but you want to be a singer and you will never forgive yourself if you let this concert pass without having a go."

"I'm not sure I do want to be a singer anymore – it's too . . ." I couldn't think of the word for a moment "it's too public."

"Cassandra, I would like to help you do this so that you have the option of continuing with it. If you eventually decide not to be a singer, then that's fine. But don't decide because you don't want to be seen in public. That's a very dangerous way to think."

"What do you mean?"

"Well, if that's too public, then so are a million other things, and you could end up in your house never venturing out. Then that crash won't just have left physical scarring, but it will have mentally scarred you too."

I was just trying to think what to say to squirm out of singing without it making me sound like I was already mentally damaged, when the door opened.

"Ah, Rob. Wonderful – Cassandra is singing *Jesu, Joy of Man's Desiring*. Here's the piano music – that keyboard is best."

I was busy pulling my hair over my face. Rob. Of all people – why was he playing? Rob Porter was tall, awkward and clumsy most of the time but set him by a keyboard and it was quite different. His playing was fantastic. He already had a place guaranteed at the Royal Academy for next term, on the strength of his Music 'A' level which he took at my age. Oh, and because of all his grades of course – on piano, tuba and violin.

I dare not sing in front of him.

I dare not chicken out either.

I stood there, face turned away from him, trying to control my breathing. I was feeling very panicky and counting to ten made no difference at all. My head was beginning to spin and I thought I might faint.

Miss Jenkins didn't even seem to notice.

"Now then Rob, Cassandra hasn't been able to practise this for a while. Her voice is a bit rough. So we'll just have a little warm up first."

I heard Rob speak behind me, "Don't worry Cass – I broke my arm playing rugby and all my practices went out of the window. I've managed to get back up to speed with a bit of hard work."

I nodded, trying to count in my head, to slow my breathing.

Two of them wanting me to sing now.

I sat down.

"Give me a minute." I said, between breaths.

They were both quiet. I could hear my breaths beginning to slow down. I gulped.

"Feeling better?" asked Miss Jenkins.

"I think so."

"Come on then, let's not waste any more time. We'll start with a scale," said Miss Jenkins.

I turned round.

Rob gave me the thumbs up sign and played a middle C.

I opened my wonky mouth and out creaked a scale, followed by another and another. It felt as if my mouth was going all over the place, I had to really concentrate to make it work properly. I must have looked terrible.

But Rob didn't look appalled. And as for Miss Jenkins, well, she just joined in.

Babysitting Monday, 19th May 8.13 PM

From: Jennings, Emma [mailto: ejj9@hotmail.co.uk]
To: cassandra briggs
Chapter28.ejj.doc

Hi Cass
I haven't read your chapter yet. Did glance though it. I realised that neither of us had written about when we were babysitting Sam. I think it was just before your music lesson with Miss Jenkins and the scrumptious Rob. I thought you might not want to write about it. So here it is.
Back to History revision. I think I missed a piece of coursework. Maybe if I do well in the exam I'll still get a C. Don't know if it works like that. But I can hope.
C u 2morrow
Luv and hugs
Em x

28

by Em

I can't remember why I was sitting for Sam. Maybe it was foster carer's support group. Susie is well into this fostering business. I think she really wants to get it right with me 'cause I'm the first teen she's had. I'm not sure if I'm meant to babysit, which is why she said it would help if you came round too. She really trusts you.

We'd done that about 3 times before then, hadn't we? We usually played with Sam before he went to bed and read him a bedtime story. Well, you did because he just loved you. After that we usually watched a DVD.

Susie was just leaving when you came and I was giving Sam his bottle. He was all sleepy. You had that hoody sweatshirt thing on and you seemed all out of breath. Susie answered the door as she went. I remember hearing her asking you if you'd been running. But you hadn't. I reckoned you'd got worried about walking round.

Anyway, there I was, cuddling Sam and you came in. It was all soft lighting in the room – just the table lamps – and Sam sat bolt upright and put his hands out to you. You took him from me and cuddled him where you stood. Then you sat down with him and turned him round and said

"How's my favourite little man, then?"

And he howled.

He put his arms out to me and I took him back.

"I expect he's got wind," I said.

But you had started to cry. That didn't make it any better. Sam hung on to me real tight and buried himself in my jumper. Then I took the risk that I might make things worse and said,

"It's all right Sam. It's Cass. She's come to see you. She'll read you your favourite *Mr Gumpy* book."

Then to you I said,

"Come on Cass. He's only a little kid. He'll realise it's you in a minute. Just act normal."

But you couldn't. And I couldn't do anything with Sam.

"Go and get us a drink Cass, and I'll put him to bed."

You stopped snivelling long enough to say

"No, don't, or he'll never like me again."

Gradually you calmed down and Sam stopped clinging so tightly. He looked at you with his great big eyes.

"Cass is sad now," I said, "Cass has got a poorly face."

You edged along the settee towards us. Sam carried on staring.

"Maybe he needs to touch your face."

"I don't think he will."

"Let's see."

"Poor Cass. Her face is poorly. Let's make Cass feel better."

I put my hand up to your face and touched your scars. I could feel the slight oiliness of your make-up and the grooved skin. You looked astounded, but didn't back away. I felt really strange, I'm not a touchy-feely person, ever – it took a real effort to keep doing it.

"Poor Cass. Let's make Cass feel better," I said again, showing him that I was stroking your face.

Sam lent forward and shot out one plump hand towards your face. His fingers just touched. You seemed to be forcing a smile.

"Thank you Sam. What a good boy," you said.

Then, do you remember what he did next? He said,

"Cass".

I'm sure that was the first time he'd said your name. You didn't have to pretend then. You were really grinning.

"Cass," he said again.

He still didn't want to sit on your lap. But he gave you his book like he did when he wanted someone to read him a story. He turned the pages till he found the one about he wanted. He pointed to the garden.

"Yes Sam. A big brown furry rabbit. Just like your rabbit," you said.

I watched as you started reading from that page. His head lolled against your arm as he became more and more sleepy again. You carried him up to bed.

Then what did we do? Oh yes, I remember. We had a long discussion. We decided Sam was not frightened of you but upset because of the scars. Now he knew it was you, he'd be fine. Then we opened the bag of popcorn and that's when we watched *Sleepless in Seattle.* That's the really gushy film about some girl who falls for a really nice man who has a little boy. They meet over the radio and they end up getting together even though they live thousands of miles apart. I think it's my favourite film out of all those old ones.

When the film was over you asked me what I was doing on Saturday. I knew you would and I knew you'd be upset when I told you.

"Susie might be taking me into Cambridge to look for a prom dress."

You sort of pulled in your breath and turned away.

"I have been looking forward to the prom since Year 7," you mumbled, "and now it's here I can't go."

"Why not?"

"Because, because of this!" You shouted, pointing at the right side of your face. I didn't know what to say. Talk about an evening of 'high expressed emotions', as Susie says.

"It doesn't matter what you look like – it's what's in your head that counts."

As soon as I'd said it, I knew I'd made a mistake.

"How could you? How could you come up with such stupid nonsense? You know it matters. It matters to me! It's my life and it's ruined."

I was thinking real fast while you were gathering up your hoody thing and a magazine you'd brought with you. I stood between you and the door.

"I'm sorry Cass. Real sorry. I said the wrong thing. Don't go."

"You have no idea, no idea at all."

"Then tell me. Tell me what it's like."

We stood there, looking at each other in the hall. I desperately wanted you to stay. I wanted to understand. You put your hand on the door handle. Then Sam gave a little cry in his sleep and I said,

"You can't go yet. You're Sam's official babysitter. You can't let Susie down."

You shrugged, and we both knew you'd stay. We walked back in the front room.

But we couldn't really think of anything much to say to each other. Something had changed between us.

Our next chapter (29!!!) Tuesday, 20 May 9.10 PM

From: cassandra briggs [mailto: cassab88@yahoo.co.uk]
To: Jennings, Emma
Chapter 29.CB.doc

Hi Em
You wrote that bit about Sam really well – you just knew how I felt. Sorry I sometimes think you don't understand. You have my full permission to tell me off and remind me about chapter 28 next time I'm feeling sorry for myself and accuse you of being unsympathetic. Or is it unempathetic when you don't know how I feel? Whatever.
Anyway, here's what happened when you needed me, for once.
Love
Cass xx

29

by Cass

That incident with Sam had completely thrown me. I know he's only a little kid, but not-quite-two year-olds don't pretend. I started to think that I must give everyone a fright. And just to make things absolutely the pits, you were hardly talking to me. I had upset my closest friend, which you are, even if you don't do 'close'. I decided I was no longer capable of anything. I was giving up.

But while all this was going on in my head, you were having problems too. You arrived on my doorstep at about 8 pm on the Thursday. This time I hadn't gone to bed – I was too busy arguing with Mum about whether I should do the school performance. She was all for it now – she'd been won over by Miss Jenkins – but I was getting more and more scared as time went on. No way did I want to stand on that stage and let everyone see my face. I just wanted to hide.

When you rang the doorbell, Mum went to answer it. She must've seen from your face that you'd been crying, 'cause I heard her say

"What's the matter Emma? Are you all right? Is it Susie?"

I came to the door of the living room. You looked awful. Your eyes were all red and puffy and your mascara was all streaked.

'I'm all right Mrs Briggs, I just need to talk to Cass."

You weren't all right. We went up to my room and between great gasping sobs you told me that you'd had a dreadful row with Susie and called her an 'old witch' then maybe something else, stronger, but you wouldn't tell me what. Then Sam had woken up and you were so busy shouting at her, you didn't realise and he was stood crying at the door. Susie had gathered him up in her arms and said over her shoulder,

"I don't care what is going on in your head, Emma Jennings, I am not going to let you upset my son. We will talk to your social worker in the morning."

After you told me this, you stopped sobbing and grabbed great handfuls of tissues out of my tissue box, then blew your nose loudly. You were screwing the wet tissues up in your hand leaving little white bits all over my magenta bedroom carpet.

"She's going to send me away, isn't she?"

The full implication of what you just said hit me. How would I cope without you? I reached for a tissue, too.

"You can't go."

"She'll make me. I upset Sam."

"No, you're good for Sam, most of the time."

"I'm awful. I can't even take care of little kids. I'll never be a mother. They'll take my kids away too."

"No, Em. They took you away from your Mum because she was on drugs."

"And that's another thing – she wants me to go back home."

I was confused.

"Susie?"

"No, my birth Mum. Kelly. I've seen her eight times in seven years, supervised by a social worker. Now all of a sudden she wants me to go and live with her when I'm sixteen. I don't even know her."

I didn't really know what to say to that.

"Well, it's nice that she wants you."

"It would be awful. I want to stay with Susie. We get on and I really love Sam."

"Wouldn't you have to leave Susie at sixteen anyway?"

"No. I have a court order until I'm nineteen if I'm in full-time education."

"But didn't you say you wanted to go into some leaving care scheme?"

"I did. But I don't want to now. I'm not ready."

You got really upset again and I tried to sort out what you'd been saying. Something didn't match up. Suddenly I spotted it.

"Listen Em. Stop and think. If there's a court order until you're nineteen, your mum can't take you back."

"She says she's going to court."

"But that will take ages. And won't they ask you what you want if she does?"

"But I won't have anywhere else to go."

"Yes you will. I expect Susie was just cross." A thought struck me. "I s'pose she knows where you are now?"

"No."

"Em – she'll be going frantic!"

I rushed downstairs. My Mum was on the phone. I signalled to her that I needed it. I knew I had no credit on my mobile.

"Just a minute," she said into the phone, "Cassandra is trying to tell me something. I'll just see what she wants."

She pressed the mute button

"I'm trying to have a conversation here, Cassandra. What's the matter?"

"I need to let Susie know that Em is here before she rings the social worker."

"Don't worry, she knows. I'm talking to her now. Is Em feeling better? Susie would like her home before 10."

I gave my Mum a quick hug and hurried to tell you.

Your mum comes up with a neat surprise

Wednesday, 21 May 6.20 PM

From: Jennings, Emma [mailto: ejj9@hotmail.co.uk]
To: cassandra briggs
Chapter30.ejj.doc

Hi Cass
Thanks for being there for me that night Cass. I thought I needed to write this bit about what happened next. You know, when your Mum told us what she'd been planning. You've got a great Mum there.
Must do some revision now. Susie said we should stop writing till after the exams. I dunno. I'm sure it's helping me. Control thing, I think. Stuff doesn't pop into my mind at other times as much. What about you?
C u at school.
Luv and hugs
Em x
You're the one with someone at school who likes you! I think you know who!

30

by Em

Do you remember? Your Mum brought us hot chocolate with cream on the top that night. But she had brought up three mugs. I thought *here we go, a lecture from Cass's mum.*

It wasn't a lecture. It was more of an offer to help. That's what she was talking to Susie about. She had rung her to say I was there and to ask her if everything was all right.

"I hope you don't mind that I spoke to her, Emma."

I shook my head. It couldn't make things worse than they were already.

"Susie told me about Sam being upset and what she said."

I shrugged.

"She says she's sorry."

I was all ears by now. In my years of being in care, my foster carers never admitted they said wrong things. They just said them and left you hurting. Then you got all angry and made things worse. Then they sent you away.

"She is going to talk to the social worker, Emma, but not about you leaving."

"What about then?"

"Well, I think it's about contact? Susie was a bit cagey because of confidentiality."

"My Mum wants me to go and live with her."

"Ah, that makes sense. Well, I think she wants to let the social worker know how upset you are."

I felt this big, big relief. I was going to stay with Susie. But there was still an uncomfortable knot in my belly.

"Did she say anything about the leaving care scheme."

"No, she didn't. But there is one other thing."

I waited, expecting bad news. I knew about 'one other thing'. It was like some great flag waving around shouting 'disaster'. Like from the head, after giving me a detention – "one other thing and you'll be excluded". Or from the social worker – "one other thing and you'll have to change placements."

While I was thinking about all this stuff, your Mum was speaking and I was hardly listening. I suddenly realised what she was saying.

"Sorry, Mrs Briggs, could you say that again?"

"I'm trying to make arrangements so that you can stay here when Susie goes away for any reason."

"What? So I can stay here when Susie has a holiday? I haven't got to go to no respite?"

Your Mum laughed,

"Well, yes, you will have to go into respite care, but if all goes to plan, it will be with us. I've already spoken to a social worker and filled in forms. There'll be an interview of course, and checks on me. But she's pretty sure I will be approved. We'll have to wait and see."

You know, Cass, sometimes having the threat of something being taken away makes you really appreciate it. Although your mum was being real nice and motherly, and was trying to do this incredible thing for me, I wanted to go back and see Susie and Sam.

"That's real cool, Mrs Briggs. But, do you mind if I go home now?" I asked her.

"Of course you can," your Mum said, "I expect Susie's waiting to talk to you".

I'm sorry Cass, if I'd known how you were battling with all that stuff in your head, I'd have stayed and chatted all night. Well, until I had to get back by 10. And I didn't know your Mum hadn't talked to you about me staying. Maybe you didn't really want me to?

Secrets and stuff Saturday, 24 May 11.35 PM

From: cassandra briggs [mailto: cassab88@yahoo.co.uk]
To: Jennings, Emma
Chapter 31.CB.doc

Hi there Em
You're right, I wasn't too pleased at first about what my Mum had done. Not because I didn't want you to stay – but here was another secret. Mum seemed to have too many of those and she sprung them on me with no warning. It was sort of making me confused – you'll see, I've written about it here in Chapter 31.
I can't believe we've written so much. It's like a book already.
Mum doesn't seem to mind me doing all this writing. She's just about given up the thought that I'll get loads of A stars in the exams. That was the old me – before. Mind you, she's still hoping I'll get good enough marks to go into the sixth form if I want to. I don't know whether I do now. I'll just be glad when the exams are over.
Better go to bed, it's late.
Love
Cass
Oh, one more thing, I know who you mean at school – but I don't think you're right. He's just a nice guy who helps everyone. But even if he does like me, I'm not free, at least I don't think so.

31

by Cass

I was going down and down. I could feel myself spiralling, like the psychologist had described once before. I tried to remember what she said about spiralling up again. Whatever it was, I couldn't do it. I pleaded with my mum not to make me go to school. I ignored all the texts Spider was sending me. I was so fed up with him – not just because of the accident, but finding him with Mum, laughing, then them both stopping. Mum didn't laugh much with me now and Spider never ever said anything funny. In fact, come to think of it most of his conversation to me was made up of 'You all right, Babe?' I was trying to block him out of my mind, but he wouldn't go.

He'd never made me feel good about myself – well, only briefly when he asked me to ride with him in his motor. Look where that led. Since then, I'd never been sure of him. Why was he still around? Did he like me? Or did he feel guilty and sorry for me and think he ought to hang about in case no-one ever wanted to go out with me again?

I knew something. I was dead scared of losing him. I hated being with him and I hated being without him.

Then there was you, Em. It's real strange but I began to feel really angry about you. There I was, needing my mum more now than ever, and it was like she would rather look after you. Maybe I wasn't good enough for her now and she wanted to have a daughter with perfect looks. Why hadn't she told me she was putting in to do respite care of you? And what was that all about anyway? Did that mean you would be my foster sister – I wasn't sure I wanted that, I needed you as a friend. Anyway, I'd never had a brother or sister.

So that's why I was a bit stand-off-ish with you. I hated not seeing you, but I told my mum that I couldn't cope with anyone and I sort of hibernated. I told her I had headaches, whether or not I had, so she got all worried about me and I was taken to the doctor. She came in with me, which was dead embarrassing – after all, I am nearly 16.

The doctor asked me all sorts of things like where the headache was and how intense it was and how long it went on. I had to be really vague with my answers – I didn't really want to lie to the doctor, but Mum was in the room and I didn't want her to think I'd been lying to her. I think he knew something was up, 'cause he asked her to give us some time on our own.

He waited until my Mum closed the door before he asked

"Cassandra, how are things going for you now?"

I knew what he meant.

"Ok, sometimes."

I didn't dare say anything else because I could feel I was welling up with tears.

"What about the rest of the times?"

"Not very good." I was really struggling now to hold myself together.

"Look, Cassandra, when people have gone through the sort of trauma you have experienced, they often need some help sorting out their lives again. I'm going to see if the hospital psychologist can offer you some more appointments. Would that be all right?"

I nodded. He called Mum back in and the first thing she did was hand me a tissue. Then she agreed I'd see the psychologist again and that was that really.

Except when I went back home I felt even worse because now I felt like a head case.

The same day you rang and asked me to come round because you wanted to talk to me about something. You'd promised Susie you'd be keeping an eye on Sam while Susie was painting the front room. I was going to say 'no' but you'd already told Mum what you were ringing for, before she brought the phone up to my room. So Mum was saying,

"You go, Cassandra, it will make a change. I'll pop you round in the car on my way to the meeting at church."

I felt cornered, but I figured it would be better to be with you, than here on my own.

"All right," I said, "if I have to. But I won't stop long".

Later, when Mum left me outside your front door, I waved to her as she went. I'd been thinking about how Sam was when I first saw him last time. I couldn't bear him doing the same thing again. So I was dithering on the pavement thinking about turning round and walking, only you opened the door with Sam in your arms.

"Hi Cass," you said.

"Cass!" said Sam, with his high-pitched voice. He nearly fell out of your arms trying to reach out to me. I took him from you and rubbed my face against his hair – it smelt gorgeous, all baby shampoo-ed.

"I've just given him his bath," you said. "We'd best get him back in the warm."

I took him in to the hall. The house smelled of fresh paint. Susie called out from the front room,

"Hi Cass, don't come in – I'm on the ladder behind the door."

"Hi Susie."

You'd started to go upstairs – Sam was squirming to get out of my arms so I put him down and we both climbed the stairs on all fours. For just a minute or two I felt normal. Well, just until I went into your bedroom.

I used to think it was great the way you had posters up all round your room – but before the accident I'd never even looked at them properly. Now I was in a room surrounded by pictures of beautiful people. The boy bands were fine – but it was the females that made me squirm. Jennifer Aniston, Kate Moss, Naomi Campbell. I stopped looking. I felt awful.

"What's the matter?"

I couldn't tell you – I couldn't expect you to take down all those posters just because I had an ugly face.

"Oh, nothing. I'm just having a difficult time at the moment."

"Well, let's get this young man to bed and then we can talk about it if you like."

"Talking won't help."

"Then we'll dance, or sing or whatever it takes."

She did a little 'la, la, la' twirling around.

Sam went "La, la, la" and toddled in a little circle, clapping his hands.

He looked so cute.

I clapped as well,

"Clever boy, Sam."

I sat down on the floor cushion beside him and he scrambled onto my lap. He snuggled up to me and pushed his thumb into his mouth.

"Story time, I think. Do you want to do the honours?" you asked.

So I ploughed into reading something from his 'In The Night Garden' book and Sam joined in every now and again, saying "Ninky Nonk" and "Upsy Daisy".

"They're his favourites, I think," you said. "Although I don't think he has a clue what it's all about."

Susie knocked on the door, then appeared round it. Her blond hair was pulled up in a ponytail band and she had a coffee coloured splodge of paint on her nose. She was wearing a very paint-covered pair of dungarees.

"I've got Sam's bottle here – how's my handsome boy?"

Sam snuggled in her arms and she sat on the bed giving him his bottle. He was too tired to drink it really, so she soon gave up and carried him through to put him to bed. You stood up and collected up the books.

"Well, I guess that's my duties over. Do you want to stay here, or shall we go to your house."

"No, I'm all right here now."

You looked round the room in a puzzled way. Then you realised.

"Would you like me to take the posters down?"

"No – it's cool. I'll cope."

Chapter 32 Our agreement

Monday, 2 June 8.01 AM

From: Jennings, Emma [mailto: ejj9@hotmail.co.uk]
To: cassandra briggs
Chapter32.ejj.doc

Cass
Just finished writing this, about the pact, but need to rush. I'm a bit late and I've got an exam. Woke up at 6 this morning, remembering our conversation. So I felt like I had to write it before I forgot.
C u l8ter
Luv etc
Em

32

by Em

I'd invited you round for a reason, Cass, and it was time I got on with what I wanted to talk about. It took me a few minutes to think what to say.

"About Spider," I said.

"What about Spider?"

"He keeps texting me to ask if you're ok."

"Well, I'm not."

"That's what I told him."

"Have you dumped him, Cass?"

"No. Not really."

That's when you told me all about him telling you to put on your make-up, then coming home to find him laughing with your Mum and – what's worse, stopping when you came in.

"He's out of order," I said.

"So's my Mum."

"No, I meant about what he said about your make-up. He should accept you as you are."

That started you off. I suppose it was your turn to cry over me 'cause I cried on your shoulder after that row I had with Susie.

"No-one will be able to accept me like this," you said.

"They will Cass. I'm sure the right person will come along." Me and my stupid clichés. You looked real angry.

"I hate it when you come out with stuff like that."

"I'm only trying to help. Anyway it might be true."

"How do you know? You have absolutely no idea how I feel. You simply do not know what it is like to be me."

"I do know what it's like, Cass. I really do. I've done heaps of thinking over the past few days. I think I've figured it out. You're the other way round to me."

"What?" you shrieked.

"Sh. You'll wake Sam. Then we'll both be in trouble. Sit down and I'll tell you what I mean."

You picked up my floor cushion and for a moment I thought you were going to throw it at me. You didn't though. You just threw it down on the other side of the room and plonked down on it.

"Well, what exactly are you trying to tell me?"

I went carefully. I did not want to lose you as a friend. So I thought about every single word.

"I look more or less ok, right? No scars."

You nodded.

"But I've had a real awful past with my mum on drugs and the social taking me away, and then all those foster carers. And the man that did those things. You know."

You nodded. We'd talked about all that before.

"So you're scarred on the outside but sort of all right inside. And I'm sort of ok on the outside but scarred inside."

"We're both damaged goods," you said.

"No we're not just that. We've both been through stuff. We've both survived stuff."

"I'm not sure I'm ok on the inside," you said.

"And when I get real angry or hit people, my hurt from inside comes outside. So I'm not quite all right on the outside, either." I said.

We both sat there thinking, for a bit.

"Do you think we'll get through it?" you asked.

"We've got to. We can have a real go at it, you know. Or we can just sort of give up."

You went quiet for a moment. I thought you were thinking through what I'd said. You weren't looking at me. You were pulling threads out of my beanbag.

Then you dropped a bombshell.

"I feel like killing myself sometimes," you said.

Well, Cass, I'd felt like that before. But I never expected you to say it. You always seemed sort of calm. I thought real fast about what to say next.

"Is that the answer? What happens if you do that?" I said, expecting you to say how upset your Mum would be.

"I don't know. Some people think it's a terrible sin and you go to hell."

"Do you believe that?"

"I don't know, I always think of God as good and forgiving."

"But is there a hell?" I said.

"There's a hell all right, I'm trapped in it now."

"No you are not, Cassandra Briggs! You are in a bad place but it's not hell."

"It feels like it."

"Ok – well, I'm no Vicar of Dibley, but I thought hell had nothing good. You've got a great Mum, a fab Dad and me. Your best mate, I hope. And you've got a good brain. And that's before all the things like your nice house. And you've got all your instruments to play. And that funny church you and your mum sometimes go to where you sing all those funky songs."

I was running out of good things.

By then you were crying. I don't do hugging – I find it real difficult, unless it's a little kid, so I sat there stroking your arm. I just waited, handing you tissues, like Susie did with me whenever I was upset. I was thinking all the time about what to do next.

"Feeling better?" I asked. You nodded.

"We're going to make a pact," I said.

"What do you mean?"

"We are going to make a formal agreement. We'll support each other and help each other grab what's best in life. We are going to make sure we take any opportunities that come our way."

"Are we?"

"Well have you got a better idea?"

Susie came in a few minutes later, having finished her painting. She found us on the computer trying to put together a contract. I felt a bit embarrassed explaining it to her, but she seemed quite impressed we were doing it. We both signed it and Susie offered to witness it for us.

It went like this:

"We, Cassandra Alicia Briggs and Emma Jane Jennings, do hereby agree that we will from henceforth consider ourselves as survivors, not victims, of our past experiences. We further agree that we will support each other in all efforts to show others that we will not be held back by these experiences. We will encourage each other in believing in ourselves and in any one or anything that will help us to overcome what has happened. We will take every opportunity that comes our way to enhance our futures. If opportunities do not arise we will create them.

Signed: Cassandra Briggs Emma Jennings

Witnessed by: Susan Bolton"

It might not have been the right moment, but I asked you then what I asked you before:

"Please Cass, would you come to help me choose my prom dress?"

"You are so crafty, Emma Jennings. Fancy asking me that when I've just signed our pact!"

"Well, will you?"

"I don't know, I'll think about it," you said.

Dresses! Monday, 2 June 7.59 PM

From: cassandra briggs [mailto: cassab88@yahoo.co.uk]
To: Jennings, Emma
Chapter 33.CB.doc

Hi Em
Read your chapter about our pact and then got to thinking. Were you planning the contract before I came? I bet you were. I haven't felt like killing myself for ages – I'm so glad I don't get as low as that now.
I've written about our outing to Cambridge for you to look at prom dresses. I still don't know how you got me there! You definitely have the power of persuasion.
Has Susie booked her holiday yet?
C u 2morrow at school.
Love
Cass

33

by Cass

By the time Saturday arrived you had talked me into going with you and Susie. Mum came too. I was scared. Scared that people would stare at me, scared of my feelings about you buying a prom dress when I wasn't going. That knot of fear in the middle of my stomach just would not budge.

On the way, in Susie's car, Mum sat in the front and we could hear her and Susie chatting about the respite thing. I felt really squirmy and uncomfortable. I hadn't spoken to you about how I felt, nor had I told Mum.

"I hope it all happens, Cass. It'll be so nice to have someone I really like to go to. I hate it when Susie has a break – they send me off to anyone who has a place."

"Yeah."

You glanced at me.

"You are ok about this, aren't you? It's only about four weekends a year and maybe a week in the summer holidays. I won't be any trouble."

How do you always guess what I'm thinking?

I laughed, hoping it sounded genuine.

"I'm sure we'll have a great time," I said.

We were going into Cambridge, to start with a shop near the Grafton Centre that Susie had been told about. A sort of boutique, not a charity shop at all, which is all you had expected. Susie left the car at the park'n'ride and she and my mum were chat, chat, chatting all the way in on the bus. I had only been on a bus a few times since the accident. This one was really crowded. I just knew everyone was looking at me. I felt more and more self-conscious and kept pulling at my hair. It was a really warm day but I wished I'd worn my hoody.

You were busy telling me all about your child development project. It sounded like you definitely deserved the good mark you got, but I'm sorry I couldn't feel enthusiastic about it. I was having trouble just coping with being out and about. Maybe you were just rattling on to try to distract me, I don't know.

When you told me all about the shop, I imagined this huge place where I could disappear behind racks of clothes and no-one would notice me. I was not prepared for the tiny little boutique with the jingly bell, round in the backstreets.

"I'll wait outside." I said.

You gave me that 'don't do that' look you'd been using ever since we'd signed that pact.

"Please come in Cass – don't leave me with them!"

Mum and Susie were already in the shop making funny sort of whooping noises which, when the door was opened, turned out to be cries of delight.

"Susie, look at this, isn't it pretty?"

"Marian, have you seen this dress, it's gorgeous, and a little bag to match."

The shop owner, or manager, or whatever she was turned and smiled as we came in. I made sure she couldn't see my face and looked for a corner to hide in. There was nowhere. The little shop was crammed with racks of dresses round the side and low displays of bags and shoes on tables in the middle. I pretended to look at the racks of satin ballgowns, or whatever they were.

"Now young ladies, prom dresses is it? Let's have your sizes and I can show you what I have for you."

"Just one prom dress," said my Mum. "My daughter doesn't need one."

"It's for me," you said. "They're just helping me choose. I'm about a size 8 or 10." Your voice sounded bubbly and excited.

"This side then – let me see – this one would look gorgeous on you." She pulled out a peach coloured dress. I felt very relieved I wasn't buying one. I thought it was an awful colour.

"No, not my colour," you said.

"I think Emma would prefer a purple, or a deep turquoise, something like that?" said Susie, looking at Em to check she was right. Em nodded.

The sales lady pulled out about eight dresses. They were all stunning. Susie started to look at the prices.

"Not these three, I'm afraid Em. See if you like any of the others."

"But this one is over £100," you said, holding up a dark turquoise full-length dress, "you'd better put this one back too."

Susie laughed. "You won't find one much cheaper than that!"

You and Susie had a little whispered conversation. Then I heard you say "are you really sure?"

After that you were away. You tried on four dresses, three of which looked fantastic. They were all too long of course – but the sales lady had 'a little lady round the corner to do alterations' and a special offer, so that there would be no charge. She found you a pair of silver glittery high heels to wear (marked £185!) to try them on. Then out came a few tiaras – we didn't look at the price, and all the little bags and other accessories.

You just stood there, letting Mum and Susie and the sales lady admire you and dress you up with all the accessories, then back into the changing room in the next dress and off again being accessorised. We were there ages. I preferred you in the paler turquoise one, but you settled for the darker turquoise because you couldn't choose and it was cheaper. My legs were killing me, standing around like that. The sales lady saw me moving from foot to foot and produced a chair. I was sat right by the bargain bin. Just for something to do, I started to rummage through it. Most of it was the sort of thing that no-one would buy – a sequin covered handbag with a clasp that didn't quite clasp and a shawl with a fringe tassel missing. There was a green dress at the bottom of it – I pulled it out to have a look thinking Em might like it. It was a size 10. It was a very straight halterneck, made from some sort of smooth fabric that slunk across my hand following its shape, as I held it. As I turned it around, inspecting it for snags or missing straps, the colour subtly changed. There were all sorts of blues in this lovely deep, deep green.

"Look what I've found, Em."

"No, that's too slinky for me. It would look great on you though, Cass."

It was awesome. I put it across my lap and ran my fingers across the shimmery material. *I could wear this for my performance.* The thought startled me, and I neatly folded the dress and put it back in the bin.

"Why don't you try it, Cassandra?" Mum was leaning over me, her eyes glistening. I suddenly realised how important it would be for her to have me doing something normal, choosing a prom dress. But I could not go to that prom. I wasn't even sure I could sing on the stage for my GCSE.

"If it's not too expensive, I could wear it if I ever do a performance. In the future I mean," I said.

The sales lady immediately sprang into action – she took no notice of my face, but held up the dress, gently shaking it, revealing its wonderful changing colours. Before I could think about it again, I was ushered into the changing room. I was wearing all the wrong underwear for this sort of garment and I couldn't do the zip on my own, but she was there, zipping and tucking in straps and turning me round to face the mirror. I pulled my hair over my face before daring to look.

Em was behind me, smiling.

"Cass, you look incredible in that."

"It certainly shows off your lovely shape," said the sales lady. "It could have been made for you."

My mum was stood with her hands over her mouth and her eyes full of tears, just looking and looking at me.

You know, from the neck down, I looked fantastic. The halter neck tied behind my neck in a soft bow, leaving the long ties hanging down my back. At the front, the V showed a little bit of cleavage, but not an indecent amount, then the dress clung as it fitted down over my hips. It wasn't quite as straight as it looked when I held it up, but it just gently flared, hanging beautifully. It was an incredible dress, but I wasn't sure. The sales lady was fussing around me, trying to accessorise it with a tiara in my hair – I certainly wouldn't wear that for the performance – but I did try on a pair of very, very expensive shoes with it. I looked at the finished effect and turned a few times in front of the mirror.

"I'm not sure, Mum. I'll feel too exposed showing all this flesh on the stage."

"There's a little shoulder shrug to match," chirped the sales lady, "if it's not reduced already, I shall reduce it for you."

I tried the shrug. The dress still looked great with my shoulders covered. The shoes were wonderful, too. The heels must have been about 5". They were so elegant.

"Sorry, Cassandra dear, you're not having the shoes as well," whispered my Mum. "They are nearly twice the price of the dress."

She was bubbling over, though. If I had really pushed, she'd have bought those shoes. But, hey, she hadn't come out to buy anything.

Two hours later we were on our way back in the bus to the park'n'ride. By then you had found the bits and pieces to go with your prom dress from a really cheap accessories shop and we had both bought shoes. If my mum wanted an ordinary teenager, she got one! I so completely got into the buying clothes bit that I quarrelled with her about which shoes I should have when we were in about the fifth shoe shop. I ended up with very pretty silver sandals with a quite high wedge heel, although what I really wanted was the super high stilettos.

So that's how I ended up with a not-quite-prom dress. I still wasn't going to be persuaded to go to that prom, though. But I just might do my performance. Maybe.

Chapter 34 – a rehearsal & performance

Wednesday, 4 June 1.30 PM

From: cassandra briggs [mailto: cassab88@yahoo.co.uk]
To: Jennings, Emma
Chapter 34.CB.doc

Hi Em
I've written again because I had a bit of spare time, well, time when I couldn't face any more revision. I'm all revised out!!
I don't think there was much else that happened before this, was there? If there is, then we can always sort out the order later.
I haven't got another exam for nearly a week. When is your next one?
Love
Cass

34

by Cass

Over the few weeks I'd been back to school, my fringe had grown quite a bit. With the right amount of mousse and about 10 minutes of hair straightening, I could almost completely cover the right side of my face. I reckoned I might be able to manage on the stage, as long as I could stand with my left side to the audience. But, when I went for my rehearsal in the hall I nearly died – someone had moved the piano across.

Miss Jenkins was late. She ran in shouting,

"Cassandra, we're running behind, please carry on." She was out of breath and looked rather panicky. Not a good moment to ask her anything.

I took a deep breath and went up the steps. I put my music on the stand. Rob was already sitting at the piano. I hadn't seen him since the day of my first individual lesson with Miss Jenkins.

"You ok there, Cass? Still Bach's *Jesu,* isn't it?"

"Yes," I said, to his second question, but he launched straight into the intro. I missed my entrance – he shrugged and shouted "Sorry" as if it was his fault. This time he waited, and I turned the music stand round, so that my scars pointed backstage.

"Sorry Cass, didn't give you time to get ready. All right now?"

I nodded and his confident notes prepared the way. I could see the top of his head as he bent over the piano, his glossy black fringe catching the light as he moved.

I sang it to him. My voice stayed steady and sure, I lost my self-consciousness as I sunk into the music. For those minutes I was Cass, unblemished, free, my voice rising with the passion of those old religious phrases flowing from fluid vowels.

There was a moment after we finished when Rob looked up,

smiled and nodded. *I can do this* I thought. Then I became aware of myself again and pulled forward my hair. Miss Jenkins had started to clap.

"Bravo, Cassandra. If you do it like that on Friday it's a certain A. But could you face the audience? It doesn't look quite right for you to be staring at Rob while you sing this particular song."

I became flustered.

"No, I, well. I'm not sure."

Rob stood up from the piano.

"I think it helps her to be less nervous, Miss Jenkins. Is that right, Cass?"

I nodded, desperately hoping Miss Jenkins didn't think I had some sort of crush on Rob.

"Oh, I see. Well yes, stand like that then, if you have to," she paused, her head inclined, " or would it help to have the piano on the other side?"

"Yes, it would. Thank you Miss Jenkins."

"Well, I don't know who moved it, but I prefer it the other way round anyway – so let's just put it back over there!"

I couldn't very well refuse to help, so I had to put up with Rob and Miss Jenkins seeing my face when my hair fell away from it as we all three pushed the piano. It wasn't too bad though – I was finding out that once someone had accepted me as I was, or tried to help, I worried less around them.

"Careful, Cass," said Rob, "don't go breaking your hip again."

Why did that make me blush? I don't know. Maybe I had just overexerted myself with all that pushing. I liked Rob but not in that way. He was out of my league, as Miranda would say.

Which reminds me, that was the same day that you had your rehearsal for your performance, wasn't it? You had quite a skirmish with Miranda then, didn't you? You know, that made me feel better – sort of. I'm not being cruel, but it had felt as if Miranda's hate had seemed directed at me and when she was so awful to you it made it less personal. You know what I mean. Anyway, she came off worse in the end. But that's your story – back to my bit.

We had our music performance on the Friday. I woke with a sore throat and Mum busied herself around me with lozenges and lemon and honey drinks and things. I even did one of the steam things that was in Miss Jenkins' booklet, over a bowl of hot water. I got really cross with all Mum's fussing, but now I think she was just anxious for me. I don't know why I'm always so mean to my mum.

Our concert was a proper performance. Tickets had been sold and the mayor had been invited. Mum had two friends from work going and Dad came down from Leeds with Tanya. Talk about over-the-top for a GCSE.

But the dark green evening dress made me feel fantastic. I've never worn anything else before that felt so good. It rippled against my body as I moved and when I had slipped on the sling-backs earlier, they just took me up the couple of extra inches I needed. I was glad Mum made me get the wedges, because when I walked in them they were quiet. I hadn't thought of that in the shop when I'd been fighting for those higher ones. I may tell her she was right, someday.

Anyway, I was number four on the programme. Quite a good place for someone like me whose nerves build up. The piano was on the correct side, my fringe was over my face, my make-up had gone more-or-less right and my parents were sat several rows away from each other. Polly was number three – and she was playing a rather fast jazz piece on the piano. Some Brubeck; *Take Five,* I seem to remember. Her timing was great, although one or two of the notes were a bit, well, idiosyncratic is the word! The audience loved it, nodding and foot-tapping as she injected great energy into her playing. I became worried that people who so obviously enjoyed Brubeck might not like Bach.

I checked through my sheet music and that's when I realised there was a page missing. I was actually down on my knees looking to see if I'd just dropped it when they announced me. I stood up, brushed the dust off my shimmery beautiful dress and walked on stage hoping that no-one would notice I was shaking. I arranged the other pages on the stand, double-checking for page 5. No, it definitely wasn't there. Could I remember it?

At the piano, Rob was looking at me – poised and perfect in an elegant evening suit. He was waiting for me to give the signal to start playing the intro. I gave a little cough, then tugged at my hair over the right side of my face and nodded.

By then words of *Jesu* were spinning round my head. I couldn't think of their order. I felt sick. I'd forgotten the tune. I didn't know when to start singing.

As Rob started to play, so my nerves subsided. Without even trying, I found my voice coming in on cue as the words unjumbled in my mind so that I hardly needed the pages in front of me. I stared into the dark auditorium and projected my singing – monitoring the pace, the level, the rhythm, the mood. But I was assessing myself all the time, criticising myself, worrying. Where was that "I am Cass" feeling that had found me in rehearsal?

I finished. There was a pause. Then applause. I forced myself to smile, then bowed a little and lifted my hand towards Rob. In response he stood. I was so disappointed with my performance, I was struggling not to cry. We bowed again together. Then I turned and walked off the stage as calmly as I could.

"Well done," said Rob, "that was even more slick than rehearsal. You're an excellent performer."

"It was rubbish." I said.

"I don't think so, why'd you say that?"

I shrugged and turned away. How could I tell him that the joy had gone? I used to love singing so much and now a performance was just one more hurdle to try to get over. One more battle to fight. I knew I would never, ever be a singer. Anyway, even if I had the best voice in the world, who would want someone on stage who looked like me?

Coping with exams – well trying to

Wednesday, 4 June 6.31 PM

From: Jennings, Emma [mailto: ejj9@hotmail.co.uk]
To: cassandra briggs

Hi Cass
So that's why you were so quiet. You know, when we were all round at your house later. I thought it was because your Dad had brought Tanya.
I'm well tired because of exams. I'm getting all stressed out. Can't really get my mind round writing stuff. If you want to write some more then that's ok. I'll do some after History and French. That'll be next week.
Only two weeks to the prom. Please, please come. You'll regret it forever if you don't. You can wear your gorgeous dress. You look awesome in it.
Luv
Emxx

Chapter about Spider and Mum plotting

Thursday, 5 June 1.54 PM

From: cassandra briggs [mail to: cassab88@yahoo.co.uk]
To: Jennings, Emma
Chapter 35.CB.doc

Hi Em
Ok – I've written something – here it is.
I wasn't upset about Tanya being there, although I think Mum was a bit rattled. Her voice goes super-posh and she is over polite to her! She hardly talks to Dad at all around Tanya. You could cut through the atmosphere!
Not as bad as the atmosphere between us, though – awful, wasn't it? ☹
Bye 4 now.
Love
Cass
Hope your revision and exams go ok. ☺

35

by Cass

When I got back from spending the Thursday of half-term with you, I could hear laughter in the kitchen again. Spider and Mum. The same abrupt stop of conversation as before. Mum and Spider looked at each other.

"Well are you going to tell her, Stephen, or shall I?"

My heart dropped, while they started a 'no you tell her', 'no you'. My Mum seemed almost, well, *flirty*. It made me feel sick.

"I'll tell her," said Spider.

He turned to me, took a really exaggerated deep breath in and made an announcement.

"Your Mum and me are planning a party for your sixteenth birthday in July. It was going to be a surprise, but your Mum said we'd better tell you 'cause you don't seem to like surprises at the moment."

I just gaped at them. In one way it was really nice – but in another, terrifying. But Spider doing that for me? Spider never did anything for anyone. And I didn't know how I felt about Spider. Although he'd visited lots and called himself my boyfriend, we hadn't exactly been acting as any sort of couple – you know, romantically.

"I don't know if I can cope with a party." I said, trying not to let my voice wobble.

"I knew you'd say that," said my Mum "so, I don't know what you think, but we wondered about fancy dress so that everyone comes dressed up."

"Yes, Babe, I've got it all figured out. You can wear a mask!"

I looked at him aghast. I was meant to be pleased about that? My own party, presumably with my own friends, and I had to wear a mask? A disguise? Why did no-one understand?

I turned and went up to my room.

The music I put on was so loud that I didn't hear my Mum knock, if she did. I was sitting on my bed writing *accept me, accept me, accept me* over and over again in my notebook. Mum's arm went round my shoulder.

"I do accept you. I do. Please believe me Cassandra. There won't be a party if you don't want one."

Here it was again, that feeling of wanting to be a little kid. Of wanting my Mum to make it all right. But no-one could.

"Has Spider gone?"

"No, he's waiting to see if you'll speak to him."

"I don't even know if I like him, Mum. He was the cause of all this." I touched my scars.

"I can't tell you what to do, Cassandra. But I think he genuinely likes you. Maybe you should tell him how you feel."

"I can't Mum – I just can't."

"You could try – just see how you go."

I shrugged. Everything just felt like a huge effort. I was tired of it all. But something had to be done. Heaving myself up from the bed I followed Mum downstairs.

Spider was sprawled on the settee watching TV. He switched it off – stretched lazily then stood up and came over to me. He lightly touched the left side of my face.

"Your make-up's all smudged, Babe." He said it softly, almost caring.

"I know. I got a bit upset."

My Mum walked quietly into the kitchen and closed the door behind her. The air felt electric.

I could feel Spider's hand move round until it was stroking the back of my hair.

"I didn't mean nothing by the mask, you know. It just seemed good – like, you know."

Then Spider put his arms around me. I'd so wanted a real boyfriend that I felt myself sort of melting towards him. My back tingled as his hands caressed me. He turned me a little sideways to him and started to gently kiss the left side of my face. I slightly turned my head to look him in the eyes, wanting to kiss him. He paused and pulled away, just a bit. In that moment, I knew. I knew without any doubt at all that the scars would always be between us.

I stepped back. I held both his hands in mine.

"Spider, it is really, really kind of you to organise a party for me. And you have been great visiting me in hospital and pretending you were my boyfriend and everything. But..."

"Babe, is this the brush off?"

He lifted one of my hands and kissed it.

I looked at him. His face was gorgeous and he was so fit. The way his hair flopped made me long to touch it. His deep brown eyes now were large, the pupils huge. What was I doing? Most of the girls in our year would give anything to go out with him. I couldn't do it – I simply could not send him away. Maybe he could change.

"No, well . . . no. I'm just saying that if we are together, you will need to come to terms with my face. Not just pity me and want to cover it up, but accept it."

"I have Babe, honest I have."

"I don't think you have Spider, not really. Anyway, I've got to sort out my feelings about you. It's all sort of complicated."

"Why? Is there someone else?"

I laughed. *Chance would be good*, I thought.

"No – I mean with all I've been through. You know."

I just couldn't bring myself to say what was charging through my mind. What I kept trying to shut out. *Because you caused a crash that took away my face. I hate you for that.*

When you came round later, Em, I was in a real state. Spider had said he 'had to go' but then said 'see you tomorrow' as he went. I didn't know what to think about it all.

You dragged me up to my own bedroom. Plonked me down on the bed and lectured me. Do you remember what you said? It was something like this:

"Listen here, Cassandra Briggs. That boy will never be able to accept you because he is too vain. The only thing he cares about is what people think about him. Everyone seems to have forgotten it was all his fault. They're all saying he's fantastic to stick by you."

"But he is – lots of boys would have just walked away from me."

"And have you ever wondered why he didn't? You weren't even an item."

"Maybe he really likes me."

"I don't want to hurt you Cass, but I don't think Spider likes anyone but himself. He just wants to look good. You know, like some sort of hero."

I didn't want to hear this, not one bit.

"Maybe he is?"

"Well, what do you think he'll do when everyone has forgotten about the crash? I think he will ditch you and go off with some tart with no brain. In fact, you can be sure of that."

I was really angry with you. You were saying that anyone who stuck by me was only there because of what other people thought of them. Did that include you then? Were you only being my friend because you wanted everyone to think you were fantastic?

For that moment, I did not ever want to see you again.

"I think you'd better go home. And you can forget our stupid pact."

How I felt Monday, 9 June 9.03 PM

From: Jennings, Emma [mailto: ejj9@hotmail.co.uk]
To: cassandra briggs
Chapter36.ejj.doc

Hi Cass
History and French exams finished! You know, I couldn't wait to get back and start writing this. Strange that, you'd think it was too much like hard work.
Thanks for the last chapter, even if it wasn't very nice for me to read! Here's my bit about what happened next.
One week for you to decide to come to the prom. You could always leave early if you hated it. Please come!
I'll talk to you about it tomorrow.
Luv & hugs & lots of pretty pleases ☺
Em x

36

by Em

You told me to leave, so I did. I didn't know what was happening. You had become really awkward to be around. There was absolutely no pleasing you.

I had known about the party. I thought it was well nice that your Mum wanted to do it. She had even booked a hall. Spider got to me though. He was always smarming round your Mum and trying to please her. And when I talked to you I was being dead honest about his attitude. He was telling people that you needed him and wouldn't cope without him. The girls kept saying how lovely he was to stick by you.

But what I was talking to you about was Spider's attitude. Not mine. We had been friends from the first day I appeared in school and you were told to show me round. I really liked you because you spoke to me like I was anyone else. You were obviously shy, but you asked me normal things like what foods I liked. Not the usual – "how long have you been a foster child then?" Or even "Why have you moved then? What did you do to make your last people send you away?" Yes, people have asked me that on the first day when I've arrived in a new school.

You stuck by me, too. I know you hadn't got a best mate or anything, but there were loads of girls who liked you. You were quite popular with people from other years in the school, too. I expect that's because you knew them from choir, or that Christian group or something.

I remember thinking you were real posh because you spoke nicely. Then over the next few days, I realised you were brainy. You were in all the top sets for things. But you still found time to check I was all right and make sure I was included in your group at lunchtime.

You were my friend, through and through. So that's why I was so furious with you when you told me to get lost.

We didn't speak for about three days. Over the weekend it could have just been because you were busy. Or seeing your Dad or something, I didn't know. I tried to ring you on the Sunday. Did your Mum tell you I rang? I guessed you just pretended to be in the bath, and you didn't call back. Still, I wasn't prepared for Monday.

Before school, I hung about near C block where we usually met. No sign of you. I thought you must be ill or something. I was quite surprised to see you in tutorial when I went in. When I sat down next to you and said 'hello' you completely blanked me. I couldn't believe it! I'd never seen you be so rude to anyone. I pretended not to notice. All I had going through my head was 'she's been through a lot, she's been through a lot'. I was trying to give you the benefit, even then.

I chatted about anything. Like verbal diarrhoea, or something. Real random stuff. Partly to cover up and partly just to try to break you down and make you say something. But you just looked at me once, and I thought you were going to cry.

Then I did again what I had been doing all weekend. That was to play our conversation over again in my head. I was talking about Spider and how he was behaving. But I didn't think you would have reacted like that to me about someone you were not sure you liked yourself. Then suddenly it twigged what I'd said.

By then Mrs Styles was reading the register. I scribbled you a note. I can't remember the exact words but it was something like

"Just because Spider sticks by you for the wrong reason, it doesn't mean I do. We are FRIENDS Cass. We will always be FRIENDS." Only I had written it in huge letters.

You picked it up and crumpled it up, almost as if you hadn't read it. But you must have seen the massive FRIENDS. No-one could miss it. Mrs Styles had finished reading the register. People were picking up their bags and chairs were scraping on the floor as there was a general shuffling to go to their next lesson.

"Let's talk at lunchtime," I said.

"Not sure I can," you replied.

I felt suddenly very angry.

"Suit yourself," I said. And marched off to General Studies.

Sorry and Chapter 37 Tuesday, 10 June 3.15 PM

From: cassandra briggs [mailto: cassab88@yahoo.co.uk]
To: Jennings, Emma
Chapter 37.CB.doc

Hey Em
Sorry, sorry. I was so awful. Considering the circumstances, I was dead lucky you talked to me when I rang about the TV thing. Mind you, I really did have a reason why I couldn't meet you at lunchtime, if you'd let me explain! I had an extra science lesson to help me catch up with some stuff I'd missed while I was in hospital.
Love
Cass x

37

by Cass

When I got in from school that Monday, Mum flung the front door open as I walked up the path. She was jigging up and down with excitement,

"Cassandra, you'll never believe it, I've had a call from the BBC."

"Why?" I thought she must have won a competition or something.

"About you – they want you on a programme."

"Why me?"

"Apparently someone who works on the programme saw you at your performance."

"So do they want me to sing?" For a moment I had forgotten about my face – I thought this was my break.

"Well no. They want you to talk about your experiences since the accident."

I just stared at her. How could anyone imagine I would want to discuss all that in public?

"No way!" I said.

"Cassandra, it could really help someone else. Someone who has maybe gone through the same thing as you have – or something similar – but who hasn't adapted as well."

Adapted as well? I didn't think I had adapted one little bit. As far as I was concerned every day was still a struggle – to put on the make-up, to get my hair done, to put up with people's glances or stares as I went to school. To even see little kids turn away from me. No, I hadn't adapted.

"I don't think anyone could learn anything from my experience. Anyway, I'm not doing it."

I flounced into the living room and stopped short. Spider was sitting on the sofa watching the television.

"What are you doing here?" I asked, not unreasonably. I hadn't seen him since Friday when I had more or less dumped him.

"Come to see you Babe. See if we could watch a DVD or something."

I turned to my mum.

"Does he know about the TV thing?"

"Well yes, he was here."

"Don't do it Babe. You don't want people gawking at you. Do it when you've got a new face."

"What?"

So much for the acceptance we had talked about.

"Spider, this is me. This is my face. I may never, ever have any more surgery. And I will make up my own mind whether or not I go on television."

"Just giving you some help deciding."

He had. I was so mad with him I sent him home so that I could ring the BBC. I had to speak to 'Lucy' with just a number. My mother had omitted to ask her for a surname, or a job description or the name of the programme.

A very posh voice answered. I took a deep breath, and went for it.

"I'm Cassandra Briggs. I think you wanted to talk to me about coming on someone's show or something."

"Yes, I did. I am so-o glad you rang back. This is a most exciting project. It is all about those girls who have sustained facial injuries which have left them with some visible difference."

I winced, thinking she knew nothing about what it was like at all, but had looked it all up somewhere and was using all the pc language! At least she was trying to get it right.

"I'm not sure this is something I want to do."

"We-ell, it will be up to you. But this is all about having the opportunity for your voice to be heard."

"Um," nothing she said so far convinced me. She carried on,

"And it's a chance to educate others – helping the viewers have some sympathy for people who have sustained injuries so that it is easier for people to accept someone with a visible difference."

Not very promising – I hated sympathy. But she had a point about acceptance.

"What would happen?"

"You would be interviewed by Rachel Days. You wouldn't be the only one, we have contacted several other girls who have had your experience. Then we would mock up, by that I mean dramatise, what had happened to you, to provide the viewer with some insight into your ordeal. And we would like to talk to you about your feelings and in your circumstances, let me see," there was a pause – I imagined her scrolling the screen in front of her, "in your circumstances, viewers would probably like to know your feelings concerning the driver of the car you were in."

Spider – I didn't even know my own feelings about Spider.

I still wasn't sure.

"Could I be turned away from the camera? I hate people seeing my scars."

"Umm, well, I expect that could be arranged for the interview, if you're positive that's what you want, but viewers will need to see the injuries you received."

"Oh, well in that case, I'm not sure I . . ."

"Your mother said you might need some persuading! Let's see what else I can say – we-ell, we won't be filming live, so we can always cut out bits you really hate. Your mother's welcome to come along, of course, and do the interview with you. And if you are asked anything you don't want to answer, you don't have to. No-one will bully you, I promise."

"I'm not sure. I'll think about it."

"Well, we do have rather a tight deadline. Could you let me

know your decision tomorrow? Early afternoon?"

I told her I would let her know by then. That meant before I went to school really – and Mum would have to ring. This felt really scary. There wouldn't just be people in the street staring at me when I walked home, it would be millions of viewers. Did programmes like that get millions of viewers? I didn't know.

Mum was itching to hear what I'd decided.

"I haven't decided. I can't decide. I don't want to do it – but I can see people might need to know."

But secretly I thought there would be an awful lot of people out there who might just want to gawp at my scars.

Later that night, I couldn't sleep. I went to go and get a drink. Mum was dozing on the sofa, the television still on. The man who was speaking was in a white coat with a stethoscope round his neck – some doctor or surgeon. I sat and listened

"There are two ways of dealing with disability. One is to change society as a whole, to accept every member of that society whatever they look like or whoever they are." There were pictures of people in wheelchairs, someone with a cleft lip, and a very tall man. The doctor carried on:

"The other way is to change the appearance of the disfigured person, so that they are ordinary enough to be accepted as a normal person. Unfortunately, it is too large an undertaking to change society, that can only be done slowly by educating people little by little about people who are very different."

I found the remote and pressed the button to see what programme this was. Up came the blue lettering in the corner of the screen: "The Ugly Ones". I flicked off the television and marched into the kitchen, slamming the door behind me. I could not believe my mother was watching something like that!

But then, it was something like that I had been asked to appear on. I decided I needed to talk to you.

Prom! And Chapter 38 about pancakes

Wednesday, 11 June 9.45 AM

From: Jennings, Emma [mailto: ejj9@hotmail.co.uk]
To: cassandra briggs
Chapter38.ejj.doc

Hi Cass
Thought I'd jump in here and write the bit where we began talking to each other again!
As you've started saying 'maybe' about coming to the Prom, I've been chatting to Susie and she says why don't you and your Mum come round here and we can get ready together. What do you think?
Please make that a yes.
Luv & hugs
Em

38

by Em

You know, I'm not really into this getting up early, Cass. When you sent me a text and said you needed to talk to me, before school, urgently, I nearly pretended I hadn't seen it. But I had missed you so much since we fell out over Spider, that I texted you back to say come for 8 am breakfast.

And you did – well 7.45, actually, and you had to wait for me to get out of the shower. When you told me about the television programme, I was well excited.

"You can tell everyone what it's like Cass. You can teach everyone to just ignore your scars and everyone else's. You can change everything."

"I doubt it."

"Yes you can, what's stopping you? Is it the fear of people seeing your face?"

"Well, yes, that's the main thing. But I don't think I can change what people think, either."

You told me about the doctor or whoever he was on the tv programme your mum was watching. You were quite angry about your mum watching it, even though she'd fallen asleep.

"I'm not surprised she's watching that sort of thing," I said.

"Why do you say that? I thought it was appalling. It just shows she thinks I'm ugly."

"No it does not! It shows she's just trying to understand you. You want her to do that, don't you?"

You looked at me for a moment, then you nodded.

"You know Cass, there may be some people who think it's great to gawp at someone who has had an accident. There may be some who are just curious. Or perhaps looking for the best thing on the telly. But there will be others out there who really want to know what it feels like."

"Do you think so?"

"Yes. And there may be a few who have been through something similar. You could really help them, Cass."

"So if you were me, you'd do it?"

"Yep, course I would. Just for those few with good reasons for watching."

"Do you think I'm capable of doing it?"

"Well, if it's not a live programme, and you can't do it, they won't broadcast it, will they?"

"Maybe not. But I'm still not sure."

"Go on Cass – this is an opportunity. You might regret it if you don't take it."

"Well if it all goes wrong – I'll blame you!"

Then you rang your Mum and asked her to let them know you'd go on the show and we ate the pancakes Susie had cooked for us in honour of you being there for breakfast!

That answer you've been hoping for!

Friday, 13 June 3.46 PM

From: cassandra briggs [mailto: cassab88@yahoo.co.uk]
To: Jennings, Emma
Chapter 39.CB.doc

Hi Em
I forgot about that breakfast pow-wow – so I can blame you for what happened next!
Ok, I give in! I will come to the prom!!!!!
Have you been plotting this with my Mum? Last night I told her I'd decided to go. She just looked smug and said she had already bought the perfect necklace to match my dress and some clips for my hair so that I can wear the left side back from my face! I feel certain you've both ganged up on me.
I refuse to go without sunglasses, though, which have become my must-have accessory, so we are nipping into Cambridge to find a designer pair on Monday after the exam. It would be really cool if we could find some that will match the dress or the jewellery that are a bit less heavy than my usual ones.
I'm scared stiff about it, though Em. Mum says she'll pick me up at any time if it all gets too much, so I may only be there for five minutes!
Love
Cass
PS forgot to say, this is Chapter 39 – all about the TV show.

39

by Cass

I hadn't been prepared for things to go so fast. The BBC arranged it all. They organised the next day for me to come out of school, and a car to pick me up, with Mum, and take us to their Cambridge studio. I don't know if they were worried that I might change my mind.

Spider sent a text saying "All the best, Babe." I hoped he meant for the TV recording and it wasn't a goodbye. It should have been a goodbye the way I'd been towards him lately. I tried not to think about him – it was too confusing and I needed to sort myself out for the programme.

I had an absolute panic about what to wear. This was outside of my usual dress dilemmas. No-one I knew had been on TV and I didn't think there was anything at all in my wardrobe that was right.

"Wear your favourite clothes," said my Mum, "that turquoise top and your jeans. You always look good in those."

"But they're old!"

"The jeans aren't, you've had them for less than two months."

I started to argue with her about how long I'd had them – I knew they were bought before the accident even if I'd only been wearing them since Easter. That made them old to me. I was still trying to convince her when I realised I had to be ready in an hour. Not much time when you have to give your face a major makeover. So in the end I did throw on the jeans and my turquoise top, with my big brown hoody to hide in.

As usual when I rushed, my make-up wouldn't go right, so it was a real scramble to get ready and the car sent by the BBC had to wait. It was great – a limousine with black leather seats and dark windows. The smell of new leather upset me for a moment, but I just concentrated on my breathing – slow and steady – while the images of Spider's motor faded from my mind.

I had to slow my breathing again several times on the journey. Mum was really excited – talking about Rachel Days and the studio and whether the lights would be bright and how many cameras did I think there would be and should she keep her jacket on? She looked really smart in black trousers and a jade green jacket that was a little bit darker than her shirt. I felt really scruffy. In fact, I felt totally out of sorts all together. I was glad I had my shades and could pull my hair over my face.

The traffic was awful. We were quite late by the time we arrived and were immediately hurried into a small room to 'be made-up'. First problem. I tried explaining to the girl that she couldn't touch my make-up and she totally ignored me and started telling me about different bases etc that were needed for the lights, and the importance of removing any shine etc. I was getting all hot and was struggling not to cry. I was so glad my mum was there. She said,

"Now then, leave Cassandra's make-up alone, or she won't be able to go on because she will just sit here re-doing it for the hour and a half that she takes, and she'll miss the show."

There was a little discussion between two of the staff and an older lady came over.

"We'll leave it if you like Cassandra, but may I just touch it up across your nose and put a little top layer to make sure there's no shine?"

So she did – and she was as efficient as Mrs Max Factor.

Then it was meeting Rachel Days before the show. She was lovely. I was feeling really rattled by then but she talked me through what was going to happen herself. I was the first of three girls to be interviewed. The interview would take place in front of a small studio audience and then would be edited afterwards.

"No-one said anything about an audience," I said – my

stomach doing somersaults.

"Don't worry, you'll hardly see them. Just concentrate on the questions I'm asking you and answer them in whatever way you think fit."

"What about if I don't want to answer them?"

"Just tell me. If at all possible, we will move quickly on."

We went into the studio. I was visibly shaking. Rachel was right about the audience – I couldn't really see them very well because the lights at the front were bright. You know how I try to avoid lights. I was just about to pull up my hood, when I thought, *No, face up to it. Get on with it. Be a survivor.*

So I stuck my head up in the air and followed her across the front and she indicated that Mum and I should sit on the sofa opposite her. My right side was towards the audience. I stopped.

"Cassie, please could you sit there?"

Mum, bless her, spoke up.

"Cassandra would prefer to sit the other side."

There was a second or so while Rachel just looked slightly puzzled. Then she understood what Mum was trying to say.

"Sit here," said Rachel, moving off the sofa opposite.

We all changed seats. There was a flurry of people moving about the studio – then Rachel started asking me questions. No ' 3, 2, 1' – nothing. I didn't even realise we had started.

First of all she asked me my name and age. Then she briefly told the audience the facts of the accident. I was pleased about that – I had dreaded trying to talk through it without getting upset. She turned to me.

"Now, Cassie, as you know we are mostly interested tonight in how your life has changed since the accident. Especially we would like to know about how others have coped with your changed appearance. Was it difficult getting back to school?"

You know, Em, I didn't realise I had so much to say. I talked about the first day back and how I felt everyone was staring at me.

"Were the other pupils prepared for your return?" asked Rachel.

"Well, yes, but that may have made it worse. They were told I was coming back and that I would look very different. I would have a 'Visible Difference' but to treat me normally. So of course everyone wanted to see what I looked like."

"How did that feel?"

"Horrible. I just wanted to melt back into my old life and for everything to be all right again. I'd been doing all right at school, so I thought getting back to studying would have helped."

"Are you still going to school?"

"Yes, I stuck it out. I have a very good friend, Em, who has helped me. And there are one or two people who have been much better at helping than others."

"Can you give an example?"

I started to tell her all about the cookery lesson and big Sue – as I was telling it I was really hoping that temporary teacher was watching.

Rachel was laughing when I was saying about how I felt like I was committing a crime when I was only baking apple pie.

"What about other friends? Is there anyone who has caused you trouble?"

I paused to think. I didn't want to talk about Miranda, really. But I needed to say something.

"There is one group of girls who don't understand. They have made my life quite unpleasant at times. It's just one of them really, the others just tag along."

"Do you want to tell me more about how they have made your life unpleasant?"

"No."

Rachel didn't bat an eyelid.

"Well perhaps you'd like to talk about the reactions of other people out of school."

I told her how difficult it was with children, and with some people who asked me what had happened to my face, or to my eye. I told her how I sometimes wanted to hide away, but I knew that there was no future in that.

"Thank you Cassie. That is really useful."

Then she turned to my mum and asked her about how she felt. Mum's answer really upset me, in a good way. First of all she talked about how you never expect anything like this to happen and how it shatters your dreams about your child's future, then she added,

"I am really proud of Cassandra. She's had the most awful trauma in her life and it's left her scarred. But she's not letting that stop her. She did her performance for her GCSE – which meant singing in a school concert – and she is now here, talking to you. I am very proud of her."

Rachel repeated how pleased she must feel when her daughter was so obviously working at getting back into her life. Then she turned to me again.

"Cassie, one of the things you do every day is to spend about an hour or more trying to cover up your scars, is that right?"

I just knew what was coming next as I nodded.

"I wonder, would you be prepared for one of our make-up ladies to remove your make-up to show us what a good job you do?"

I felt the tears well up. I tried to stay calm. No way did I want to cry in front of millions of viewers.

"No. I'm sorry. No."

"Cassie, this is really difficult for you, I know. As you cannot remove your make-up, we would like to show viewers the medical photos of your injuries, then one post-operative and end up with one of you now. But before those go up on the screen here," she smiled warmly at us – I had recovered a bit now and gave her my lopsided smile back, "I would like to take the opportunity of thanking you and your mother for being so frank and open with us."

Then she turned to the studio audience, who I had forgotten about, and announced

"Ladies and gentlemen, Cassandra Briggs."

There was a huge round of applause as Mum and I were shown off the stage.

My brave friend, Cass, the TV star

Sunday, 15 June 4.15 PM

From: Jennings, Emma [mailto: ejj9@hotmail.co.uk]
To: cassandra briggs
Chapter40.ejj.doc

Hi there Cass
I think you were tremendous on that programme. I'm glad they didn't ask you about Spider though – that would have been awful. This chapter I've written is not only about us watching the programme but also about you and Spider!
I can't wait for the prom. I tried on my dress yesterday with the jewellery and that. I looked like someone else, not me! I think I've got everything I need – even a little glittery bag. I'm not sure I like it, but Susie says it looks 'Just the biz', so I'll probably take it.
Can I come with you tomorrow to help choose the shades?
Luv & hugs
Em x

40

by Em

These things come together quickly, don't they? For three days you were worried stiff about it. You were a nightmare to be with. All those what if questions. What if that temporary teacher was watching? What if the head sued for what you said about her? What if Miranda took offence? etc. etc.

I was there half-an-hour before the programme was due to start. I was desperate not to miss it.

Anyway, there we were the two of us, all ready. We sat on your sofa with our feet up and your Mum was keeping quiet pretending she wasn't there. She'd made a bit of an occasion of it – there was popcorn and crisps and sausage rolls and other nibbly things, with Coke to drink. It was just about to start when the doorbell rang. Your mum said,

"Who's that? I'd better send them away." Then when she opened the door we heard her say,

"Oh, Spider, it's you. You'd better come in – we're just about to watch the programme Cass was on."

You went all red when he came in the room. I don't think you really wanted him there.

We both put our feet on the floor and Spider plonked himself down between us, throwing his arms along the back of the sofa.

"How's my two favourite babes, then?" he asked

We both sort of grunted. You must've guessed what I thought about that remark, so you said,

"I'll sit in the middle." You and Spider swapped places. Spider gave me a wink – I guess he thought you were jealous. I knew you wanted to put distance between me and him in case I acted out of order. He really got up my nose.

Spider looked at the arrangement of drinks and nibbles on the table and then he said,

"Any beer, Mrs B. Or even champers. It's like a party isn't it? Cassie being on telly and all."

Your mum went all flustered. She muttered something like 'maybe after the programme'. We all went quiet as the voice announced it was starting and the music began.

The cameras covered all aspects of the studio, including the audience, before zooming in on Rachel Days, who stood, just like she does on *Crimespotter,* with papers in her hand. Then she told us all about the series and how we would hear about the people who had been involved in crime.

"That's not you, Babe. I'm no criminal," said Spider.

"Shh. Listen." We all said to him.

He'd talked over her saying, 'or tragedy, but emerged as survivors', which we saw later when we watched it again without him. Rachel Days carried on,

"Today, on this first programme of the series, we will first be welcoming Cassandra Briggs, a talented, musical 15-year old who was involved in a road traffic accident when she accepted a lift with a friend."

Then followed pictures of the car after the accident, with Rachel talking about it and a picture of Cass's face, obviously taken when she first arrived at the hospital.

I felt you shudder beside me. I wanted to hold your hand, but I don't do that closeness stuff, and anyway Spider would jeer. You leaned on me, though, away from Spider.

"Close your eyes, Cass," I whispered, I'll tell you when the pictures have finished."

You did – I gave you a poke when Rachel said,

"And now we welcome our guest, Cassandra Briggs, with her mother, Marian Briggs."

I thought you looked real calm, walking onto the stage. Like you always did it. I felt well proud you were my friend. Then the interview started, and all four of us sat very still. We watched and listened, you with your hands jammed in your mouth, leaning forward to avoid resting against Spider's arm. Spider yawning to show he didn't care what happened. Your Mum all worried, glancing at you all the time. As for me, I was on the edge of the seat, watching you on and off the screen. It was the strangest sensation, you on the telly, us watching. Electric.

You did it so well. You just answered her straight. The camera was trying to get a picture of your face, but you kept straightening your hair over your right side. You'd kept your shades on, so you looked like some filmstar. We came to the bit where she asked you if you'd be able to take your make-up off. You'd told me that upset you, but at first I didn't see any tears 'cause of the glasses. Your voice went sort of wavery though and the camera caught the shot of your mum passing you a tissue. Then, of you taking off your glasses to wipe your eye while Rachel was talking to your mum. You gasped next to me.

"I didn't know they filmed that."

The camera stayed on your face just long enough to glimpse your scars. You could see clearly that you had one eye that was distorted under it. You were shaking next to me now. It was only for a second or two and then the camera was back on Rachel as she drew it all to a close.

Next to me, you were sobbing.

"It's all right, Cass, it's all right," I said, knowing full well that if it were me I'd be cussing and shouting.

"Hey, Cassie Babe, it was great," said Spider.

I thought for one mad moment that he was congratulating you on your excellent interview, but no.

"You blubbering like that can only get you a better payout on your claim."

"What are you talking about Spider?" I asked, for you.

"Insurance, you know."

"But you weren't insured."

"Don't matter, there's this criminal injuries compensation you can get. Not that I'm a criminal."

We were both staring at him like he had two heads, or something.

"I looked it all up for you, Babe. If you make a claim you'll get some money for looking like that."

Cass, if looks could kill, you'd have had him dead and buried. But it wasn't you who spoke next.

Your mum was stood up, standing over Spider.

"I think you had better leave now, Stephen. And I do not want you near my daughter ever again. If you come anywhere near this house, or even wave to her in the street I shall have the law on you." She folded her arms and waited.

"But Cassie might want different," said Spider, winking at you.

"GET OUT, GET OUT, GET OUT!!!!" You yelled.

"Time to go, Spider," I said. I tried to sound sorry, but, well, you know I was real pleased.

He just deflated. It was so strange to see. He had run out of all his cockiness and he looked pathetic. He sloped off, quietly closing the front door behind him.

"Oh Cassandra, I'm sorry. I shouldn't have done that," said your mum.

You just went over to her and gave her a real big hug. I got that jealous feeling again. I wondered if I could ever give Susie a hug. She was my closest to a real mum.

Then you and your mum had a big discussion to work out how the crying bit got in the programme. The BBC people had seemed to be really sensitive and careful. You had been sent the final film for your approval.

"We didn't watch all of it," you said, "only the bits where I was talking to Rachel. You weren't bothered about your bits Mum."

"It's my fault, then," your mum said, and you added,

"And mine."

"Nothing can be done about it anyway," I said. "People are going to just think Cass is great to go on the telly. Anyone would get upset."

There was a knock on the door. You and I looked at each other, thinking Spider had come back.

"Oh, it's a little surprise," said Mum. "A mini celebration. Susie's coming round and I thought we'd have a Chinese takeaway. And," she paused, "I hope this is all right Cass, but your Dad said he'd drive over. He won't have seen your programme because he'll be on his way."

I don't think you minded too much. You couldn't stop grinning. I guess it's quite a special Dad that travels 150 miles for a Chinese meal!

Free as a bird? Saturday, 20 June 3.46 PM

From: cassandra briggs [mailto: cassab88@yahoo.co.uk]
To: Jennings, Emma
Chapter 41.CB.doc

Hi Em
Last night was incredible! It's been difficult not to write about it today! Now that we're writing stuff that only happened a few weeks ago, I'm finding it harder to keep the right order. Are you? But back to our writing. You were spot on with your description about what happened when we were watching my programme. This is a chapter about reactions to dumping Spider, mostly.
Love
Cassxx
PS Physics exam on Tuesday next week, and then Home Economics on Wednesday – that's my last one!!!

41

by Cass

The next day, Mum was cooking eggs for breakfast, even though it was a school day. I knew that meant she wanted to talk. Sure enough, as she put a full English in front of me, she said quietly,

"I'm sorry Cass, I shouldn't have interfered."

"You mean with Spider? I'm glad you did."

"Are you sure?" I nodded, by now I had a delicious mouthful of bacon and egg. I finished eating it before adding

"Definitely. Without you saying something, I might just have carried on."

"But I thought you really cared for him!"

"I wanted to have a boyfriend. I suppose I was just afraid of being on my own. Or of losing face with the girls at school. They think he's great."

I realised what I had said. For the first time since the accident, my mum didn't come over all protective at the mention of a face. She just carried on the conversation:

"Emma doesn't. She's never liked him. Maybe we both should have listened to her."

"Maybe we should. Do you think he felt guilty, Mum?"

"Yes I do. He always went quiet around you. When you were in hospital, all the nurses loved his sense of humour. He seemed to be such good fun. But then he'd come into your room and be quite different."

"I know. I hated it when he was laughing with you and then I came in and he stopped. I think I've done him a favour really."

"We've done him a favour!" said my mum.

I didn't expect to feel so free. I thought that I would get down over the next few days, but it was as if my confidence just grew. I decided that if I had a boyfriend, I wanted to be with someone who didn't care if I wore no make-up to cover my scars. In fact, they'd have to be able to put up with my eye as well. So it would be a very special person indeed. Someone like Rob, maybe?

I started to take my sunglasses off in class to clean them. People looked, but I didn't care. I still couldn't quite manage without them – although my new eye was pretty good, the scarring round the eye still made me feel self-conscious.

Big Sue bounced up to me on the Wednesday after the Maths exam. She had the biggest smile stretching across her face.

"I hear you've dumped Spider!"

"How did you know?"

"Your bravery has gone before you! I think you made a smart move there."

"I thought people would think I was mental!"

"Only people like Miranda – most of us have thought it was about time. You deserve someone a whole heap better than Spider."

"Well, thanks." I didn't really know what to say.

But the most embarrassing thing that day was bumping into Rob. He was just standing outside the school gates when I left. Just hanging around, with his tuba case slung over his shoulder.

"Hi Cass! How are you?"

"I'm fine thanks. How are you?"

"I'm good. Missing hearing that voice of yours."

I mumbled something or other. I felt myself go hot. I hoped I wasn't blushing.

"No, seriously. I wondered if you'd sing at a charity concert I'm organising at the beginning of September, in aid of Poverty Action?"

I remembered my school performance, and how disappointed I'd been when I left the stage. Before the accident I would have jumped at the opportunity to sing on stage. Was I ready to put myself through it now?

"Um. I don't know. Can I think about it?"

"Course you can, it's ages yet. I'll ask you again in a few weeks."

He grinned at me, then turned and ambled away. I watched him go, thinking how unlike a musician he looked. He seemed more like a farmer or something. But I liked it, the way he walked.

My performance practice Sunday, 26 June 5.47 PM

From: Jennings, Emma [mailto: ejj9@hotmail.co.uk]
To: cassandra briggs
Chapter42.ejj.doc
Chapter43.ejj.doc

That last bit of chapter 43 sort of shows you were starting to fancy Rob!! I will say no more . . . .
But Cass, get ready to be impressed! Here's two chapters!!
I've started with the bit about Miranda and the music and my performance practice etc etc. This was a week or so after you finally squashed that Spider! (Best move you've ever made, I think!)
Must rush – things to do for tonight! Guess who's coming round? ☺ I can't wait to see him! Haven't got a thing to wear.
Luv and hugs
Em x

42

by Em

I got there late for my final dance rehearsal. It honestly wasn't my fault this time. Susie already had a bit of a dodgy ankle. Just before time for school she was putting out the washing. You know how she always got up before the dawn birds to do all her laundry. Well, she went down some hole that stupid free-range rabbit of hers had dug and did her ankle in, real bad. It came up like some great mountain and I had to help her in the house. Well, I forgot all about school for ages. I just put frozen peas on her ankle and made her sit in the lounge with her foot up. Then I dressed little Sam and gave him his breakfast. Just as I had mopped the floor after he'd pushed coco-pops off the edge of the table, Susie dragged herself into the kitchen.

"It's already 8.30 – you'll be late for school, Emma. I'll see to him."

"How can you? I can take him to nursery, it'll be fine. It won't hurt for me to sort him out for one day."

Susie gingerly lowered herself onto one of the chairs. She looked awful. Really white.

"Are you sure love? I think you might have to help out a bit, it is really painful. If I rest for a while, I expect it'll be better when the swelling goes down."

"You look dreadful, Susie. You just concentrate on getting better."

I made her a cup of tea. Well pot of tea actually, because I put some in the flask thingy for later. I quickly made her some ham sandwiches. Then I stuck Sam in his buggy and ran with him to nursery. I was well puffed by the time we arrived, but he was laughing and squealing.

He was a bit late, it was gone 9 by the time we got there. Then I was worried he'd be there all day if Susie couldn't walk by lunchtime, so I grabbed Mo. Do you know her? She's Timmy's Mum who lives in the same road. I know Sam's been there before so I arranged she would take Sam back and see if Susie was ok. Then I was just about to rush to school to get there in time for second lesson, you know, the rehearsal, when I realised Susie didn't know Mo would bring Sam home. I hadn't got credit on my phone so I went all the way back to tell her.

Anyway, after all that, by the time I got into the rehearsal it was 10.30! Miranda was doing her bit, prancing around at the back of the stage. I couldn't believe my ears – she was dancing to my music! You know, the Bolero thing you helped me pick out. Well, I knew that we'd been told there were to be no two pieces the same for the performance. I think that was because the whole thing was being judged as well as the individual bits. Anyway, I went to complain.

Miss Tibbetts was on the side of the stage, fiddling with the lead to the microphone.

"Miss Tibbetts, I'm real sorry about this, but that was my music and I've been practising to it for weeks."

"Emma, if you had been here at the beginning of class, we would have been aware of the clash. Someone did mention that you were using the same music but Miranda was quite certain that you had given up on it."

"But I hadn't given it up . . ."

"Don't interrupt me. Without you here, I couldn't discuss it with you, and as the last class before the performance is almost over, I think it will be you that needs to find new music."

I was furious, 'cause Miranda knew real well what I was dancing to. I'd been working on it for lesson after lesson. She'd been mucking round with her friends and hadn't even practised her dance.

So I got a bit cross with Tubby Tibbetts and she got quite

angry with me and said that it was now definite that Miranda could have the music. She wouldn't listen to any excuses 'bout why I was late. If I'd been on time, like Miranda, it would have been different. Oh, and she needed to know the music I had chosen by Wednesday to print the programme and time was up so I was too late to rehearse. Just like that!

Miranda thought she'd got the better of me – so she was on a roll. She elbowed me out of the way as we left the hall. When I gave her a shove back she raised her eyebrows and said:

"I don't want any low-life shoving me, Lackey. I have witnesses here to show it was unprovoked." Chrissie was in tow, and that new girl Debbie. Debbie walked away. She doesn't want trouble. I think she's all right really.

You know why Miranda calls me Lackey? It's 'cause I'm a looked-after child. L.A.C. You know, in foster care. My friend Sheila, you remember her, she came into school 'bout the same time as me and was fostered too. She started calling us "We two lucky lackies". Only Miranda heard and dropped the 'lucky'. Sheila got moved away into some residential place, so I reckon she wasn't too lucky in the end.

I was meant to be meeting up with you for lunch and telling you about the rehearsal. Sorry I didn't show. At that particular moment I was probably out in the playground surrounded by about fifty nosey-parkers and shaking Miranda while Chrissie was kicking and screaming at me. Funny really, I can't believe that I was fighting someone over a piece of classical music.

Someone shouted 'Tibbetts' and all the crowd who was jeering or cheering us scarpered. Even Chrissie. I let go of Miranda and pretended I was sort of helping her, but it was a bit late, and Miss Tibbetts marched us back in. She still wouldn't listen to me, though, and gave me a detention for that evening. Not funny with Susie all laid up.

Well you know how it went. I skipped detention and went back home and Susie was completely unable to stand on that foot. She needed to go to the doctor or the hospital or something. We got Mr Roberts from next-door to take us, so I spent the whole evening in A & E with her, trying to amuse Sam. They took x-rays and she'd broken some little bone. Which is why I wasn't in school the next day, looking after her till her friend came to stay to help out.

By Wednesday, I was in a big panic about my music for Friday's performance. I knew I'd be in trouble for missing detention, so Susie had written me a long note about what had happened.

Tubby Tibbetts came and found me during registration.

"I need a word with you Emma Jennings, now."

I went out into the corridor with her – I bet the whole school could hear her yelling at me.

"What do you mean by openly defying me and not attending detention? Why were you not in school yesterday? This is the most important week for your performance and you haven't even given me the name of your music. You were late for the last rehearsal, you fight someone over music and you, once again, become the trouble-maker you were last year." Her breath was right in my face and her face was getting redder and redder.

"I gave you extra lessons to help you catch up with the class and look how you reward me!"

All the time she was shrieking at me I was trying to get a word in edgeways. I gave up, and fished in my pocket for Susie's note about my absence. I held it out to her.

"What's this – some feeble excuse?"

"No miss, but it does say why I was late and where I've been."

Miss Tibbetts read the note.

"So, you've been helping your foster mother. I'm sure the social worker could have found someone."

"I might have been moved though, Miss, and I need to be here for the performance." That was true, and something me and Susie had talked about.

I'm not sure she believed me, but she had calmed down enough so as I could tell her about A & E, and taking Sam to nursery and all that stuff.

"So you still haven't found any music?"

"I haven't really looked Miss. But it took me ages to find one I liked in the first place."

"You'll have to compromise and find something you can live with. Meanwhile, we'll need to put something in the programme today. Show me the dance and we'll put a name to it."

So there I was, feeling well stupid, dancing my bit in the corridor. Those grey lino tiles were too slippy really and I was really worried all the doors would open and everyone would start to pour out for their first lessons. It went all wrong and I was in my straight school skirt so I couldn't really do some of the moves. She sighed.

"Ok, Emma. Perhaps it will look better on the stage. See if you can find something with a really good rhythm because that's your weak point. You were speeding up and slowing down all over the place. Meanwhile, perhaps if we give it a really vague title then it will match anything."

"Dance?" I suggested.

She almost smiled. "Not quite that vague! Perhaps 'Steps', or 'Movement', something like that."

"Movement would be all right. Can you give me any ideas for the music?"

Miss Tibbetts leaned against the wall and wrote out loads of things for me to listen to. I didn't have any of them and most of them I'd never heard of. She said she'd bring in some CD's for me in the morning, if that would help, but that she *strongly suggested* I found something that evening and had a real good practice or I wouldn't even get a C.

So there I was, in a real pickle. Less than two days to go, no music and a rotten dance called 'Movement'. Bit tame after 'Expression of Bolero', which is what I was going to call it.

I felt shattered and really fed up. I had that dance all worked out and it matched the music perfectly. I knew when to put in energy and when to move real soft and careful. I had written my whole project around that dance with all the criticism and bits. I didn't know what I was going to do.

43

by Em

When I got home and told Susie all about Miranda stealing my music, we both got out our CD collections and I tried to fit my dance to anything. We played bits of jazz, classic, opera, even pop. Nothing seemed to work. That's when Susie said:

"Why ever didn't I think of it? Do what you did before and go and ask Cass!"

So I did, and when you'd stopped being angry about Miranda, you were great. We went up to your bedroom with loads of music. But we had the same problem with all the stuff you had. Only now it was even worse because I was already overloaded with bits of songs in my head. We gave up after a while and went downstairs to eat toast. Then up we went again, with a plan to shortlist CD's, finding ten with a strong beat.

It was 8.30 and all we had was a handful of CD's. There wasn't really enough room to dance to try them out properly.

"Come on, Em. Let's go and meet my mum in the Church hall."

"What for?"

"You'll see."

You then started gathering up all your instruments, from all around your bedroom. Honestly, Cass, I hadn't realised you were so clever at playing music! What did you have? Guitar, flute, keyboard. No, you didn't need that because there was one at Church. But you did take some sort of little whistley thing and your violin. I started to tease you about being a one-girl band and what did you say? Something like:

"Well, you may laugh. But what I really wanted was to learn the drums!"

Somehow we managed to carry all this stuff and we walked round to the Church hall. When we got there, several ladies were standing around chatting with cups of tea or something. You told me to wait, so I stood at the back while you went and talked to your mum. I could see you nodding and smiling together and I got that real jealous feel that I always get. I watched your mum go over to a chap who I realised was the vicar – he was wearing one of those back-to-front collars. He listened with his head on one side then he boomed out,

"Of course she can. Of course. My stage is her stage. Where is she?"

He rushed over to me,

"My dear girl, if you need the stage, just use the stage, have a practice – borrow any music". I couldn't look at you in case I got the giggles.

The stage wasn't as big as the one at school but it had a wooden floor just right to dance on. We hung about a bit while all the oldies went, then we tried out my dance to a few songs. We worked for ages on an Ella Fitzgerald thing. *Summertime,* wasn't it? It didn't really work. Then we tried with you playing all your instruments. Flutey-tooting away or plucking some clever guitar stuff. Still no good.

I gave up for a bit and just went and danced my whole routine. I kept losing the timing. You started to clap a rhythm. It was so much easier.

"I just need the beat," I said.

"You know, I once wrote a poem about a beat. A long time ago – before . . . you know." Your hand went up to your face and we both stopped and looked at each other for a second. I was looking down at you from the stage and I had a flashback thingy. I was suddenly there, by the car, looking at you with your face smashed in. I imagined the picture of the crash just fading away until we were in the present. Then I tried to concentrate on what you'd just said.

"A poem? That's no good. It would take ages to write music to make it a song."

You started muttering to yourself, so quietly that I could hardly hear. Then you almost shouted –

"Quick, pen and paper – I think I can remember it."

You did too – well most of it, enough to start.

Then you read it, almost like a rap, and told me to dance. You started off:

"The rhythm of the words
is the moving of the feet
with the shaping of the arms
and the feeling of the beat
. . beat . . . beat . . . beat."

"Stop – start again – I can add a few movements to match the words to lead into my dance"

"The rhythm of the words
is the moving of the feet"

By now I was tapping my feet on the stage as you read the poem, I raised my arms and shaped them into a smooth curve letting my own, practised dance start when you reached that bit about "the feeling of the beat . . . beat . . . beat."

Your poem was real catchy and most of my dance fitted beautifully. Just like it had always belonged. I was so glad I'd chosen contemporary 'cause it suited the rhyme. I had to change a bit to match the expression of the words. That took a bit of working out, but we did it.

We came to the verses near the end. You read:

"And my coming close to you . . ."

"Who's the you in this line? Is it a boyfriend?" I asked.

You mumbled something I couldn't hear from the stage.

"What?"

"I said I wrote it for Church. You know, the 'You' is God."

"What?"

I felt suddenly deflated. I wasn't sure I wanted to dance to something religious. I sat down on the edge of the stage –

"Pass me what you've written," I said.

I read it through, carefully, thinking about all the words again. You were pacing back and forwards. You stopped in front of me.

"Well, shall I write the God bits again, about a boy or something? I suppose I could change it."

I shrugged and read it again. You were biting your lip. I realised this poem was important to you as it was.

"It's perfect as it is, Cass. But I'll need a cross as a prop to make that clear."

So I practised it again, with you reading it, and an imaginary cross at the back of the stage. It felt all right.

Your mum came back to collect us and to lock up about 11 o'clock – we were bubbling over by then and dying to show her what we'd done. She gave us both a hug (that startled me!). Then she said thank you to me when you were gathering up your stuff. I didn't have a chance to tell her it was me that should be thanking you. You'd saved my skin. All we had left to do on Thursday was to record the poem. And maybe have a bit of an extra practice.

I was hoping like mad that Miss Tibbetts would be ok about a dance without music.

Sorry Tuesday, 24 June 10 PM

From: cassandra briggs [mailto: cassab88@yahoo.co.uk]
To: Jennings, Emma
Chapter 44.CB.doc

Hi Em
Whenever I think about your performance, I feel really guilty. I am so sorry I caused you all that hassle.
Hey – do you realise we are very nearly through the exams?
Love
Cass
Ps I bumped into Rob this afternoon. Guess what? His band is playing at the prom. If I hadn't already promised you I'd go, I definitely wouldn't be! Now I am even more nervous!!

44

by Cass

Tuesday evening went quite well – we'd recorded the poem at home, with me reading it at two speeds and then used the Church hall stage again for practice. You danced ok to the slower reading, but when I read it to you, it seemed to work even better for some reason.

I felt really awkward when you started pleading with me –

"Cass, please come and read it on stage. You can hide away, if you like, but it's so much better when you vary the pace a bit."

"No way, that's why we made a recording."

"It will be second best with the CD. If I lose the timing, I won't be able to catch up."

You were right, of course. I started to think how I would feel if you refused to help me.

"All right then, as long as I can stay out of sight."

I went to bed that night and started to worry about being on stage again. I didn't sleep properly. I didn't have the usual nightmares, but a new one about you. I dreamed I was shouting really loudly all across your dance, and the more I shouted the quicker you danced until you fell over. Then we both fell – you know, that down and down and down feeling you get sometimes in dreams.

That's no excuse, I know, because your performance wasn't until the evening – except that I didn't wake up until late and felt really rough. Mum started to nag me but I was not being difficult, I just felt really down. So she told me to get back to bed.

The television people rang again. They spoke to Mum. They said they were very pleased with the programme, and did I want to go on another chat show on the radio. Mum was meant to ring back but because I said "No way, I'm never putting myself through that again," she said she would leave it for now and discuss it when I was in a better frame of mind. I found myself thinking she really wanted a famous daughter so if I'm too ugly to be a singer then she may as well have a freak show instead.

I heard the phone go a few more times. Mum brought me up biscuits and hot chocolate at about 11. She said there had been two calls, one Radio Cambridge and one from the Fenland Gazette. I just put my head under the covers and she went away again.

I did get up in the afternoon for a bit. Then I felt tired again so I went back to lie on my bed. I must've dozed off because when I woke it was to my phone going, when you sent me that text reminding me about your performance. I then worried like mad because I kept thinking – 'look what the last performance led to' and 'I shall only spoil it for Em' and stuff like that. All those 'negative thoughts' as the psychologist would say.

It actually took me that long to remember our pact. When we wrote that, I had decided I did not want to think negatively any more. So that's when I said a prayer, pulled myself together and sent you the text saying 'ok c u there'.

It wasn't any better after that, of course. I had to wash my hair and I couldn't get it to lie right to cover the scars. My eye felt uncomfortable, so I took it out, cleaned it and put it back in. As I did so, I couldn't help seeing the blank implant it usually covered. I felt even more of a freak show than usual, because of my mood, I guess. I couldn't get my mind round doing my make-up.

While all this was going on, my mum was trying to make me eat. She had cooked some tea, and brought it up on a tray. It was spag bog, and I had already put on my white top, to match what you were going to wear. I virtually threw the tray back at Mum.

"Why have you made this, of all things? How am I expected to eat spaghetti and bolognese sauce without getting it all down my clothes?"

"It's your favourite, dear. Just trying to please you."

I was yelling at her now.

"Well, it would please me if you'd just leave me alone."

Mum did. Then I felt mean. I sat down on the bed and howled.

My mobile went and it was that second text from you.

That's when I gave up and sent the text saying I might not make it and you'd better get the CD set up. Then I felt even worse because I was letting you down.

I went downstairs.

Mum was eating her tea. I sat down beside her.

"I'm not going." I said.

"Yes you are. Emma has been a really good friend to you and now she needs you. Have a glass of milk or a drink of chocolate. I'll help you put on your make-up and we'll just have time to get there."

She was a bully, but I needed it. I had promised and I didn't want to let you down. We both knew you danced better when I was there reading it. Maybe no-one would see me, standing in the wings with the mike.

So that's why I was so late. It was just the dance before – Miranda to Bolero, would you believe it! – when I arrived. You looked so pleased to see me – you did a little silent jig with the thumbs up sign, on the spot. I barely had time to think before Miss Tibbetts announced your dance. She was holding the mike I needed so we just stood there. Then she said,

"Let's welcome onto the stage, Emma Jennings and Cassandra Briggs!"

I just froze on the spot. You said something like 'Come on, you can do it' and then Miss Tibbetts just passed me the mike and told us both to go on stage. I found myself moving forwards. You stood in the centre of the nearly empty stage under the single spotlight, your head bowed down, with your hands at your side, just waiting for me to read.

I was trembling inside, but my voice just seemed to start all on its own, echoing round the stage –

"The rhythm of the words
Is the moving of the feet
With the turning of the hands
To the rhythm of the beat . . . beat . . . beat . . ."

And then you took off, dancing with all your soul. Filling the stage with your movements.

Disaster? Wednesday, 25 June 12.58 AM

From: Jennings, Emma [mailto: ejj9@hotmail.co.uk]
To: cassandra briggs
Chapter45.ejj.doc

Hi Cass
I'd been real scared you weren't coming. I just knew my performance would be a disaster. You'll see why when you read my next bit (which I just wrote, 'cause I couldn't sleep). There's a bit of overlap here, 'cause I wanted to put about what it was like when I was waiting for you.
Nearly 1 o'clock (am!!) so I think I'd better have a quick snooze. At least I haven't got another exam tomorrow.
Happy reading
Luv and hugs (!!)
Em xx

45

by Em

I knew you'd have the wobbles about helping me – even backstage – so I wasn't too fazed when you sent me those texts. In fact, when you weren't there, Rob, who was on audio, asked me if he could have the CD you'd made, so as it was ready. I said,

"No, no need. She'll be here in person."

But inside I was real scared you might not come. That's when I sent you the next text, "Cass where r u I need u"

So there I was with no back-up plan. It got nearer and nearer to when I had to be on stage. It was Miranda's turn to dance, so I went backstage and began to warm up. I was trembling. I had been so sure you would be there, I had left the CD in my bag in the changing room. The audio equipment was at the back of the hall. There was no time to do anything. I kept thinking about every footstep of my dance echoing through the hall and all the audience just staring, in silence. And then facing Miss Tibbetts afterwards. Urrgh!

When you came through that door, back of stage, I could hardly contain myself. I was so pleased to see you. But you shrugged when I asked you if you were ready. When Miss Tibbetts announced us, you looked horrified. I didn't think you'd go on stage. Neither of us moved until she came over and thrust the mike in your hand and said,

"Off you go girls."

Good job she did, because it made you move onto the stage and the audience clapped like mad and we were off. We were both a bit slow getting going, but then it just went smooth as smooth right to the end. Then I stood up and the audience applauded real enthusiastic-like. It was awesome!

I held out my hand towards you to get you to come up for a bow. I took no notice when you shook your head but I just stood and waited. No way was I going to take all the credit myself. It seemed like forever while I was waiting, but then Miss Tibbetts went and talked to you and took the mike from you. So finally you came on stage.

When we came off after the second bow (or was it the third?), I was bubbling over. I don't know if you were. You looked a bit shakey but the audience were still clapping even when we'd gone right offstage. We looked at each other and it was really funny when we both said at the same time

"You were great!"

Then

"Snap".

By now, Miss Tibbetts was saying thank you to us and stuff about us having talent and I felt all tearful because of what you'd been through and how you'd helped me so much. I felt all these strange emotions welling up inside me. That's why I did something I never ever, ever do.

I gave you that hug.

Just a little hug. You looked a bit surprised.

I don't do hugs. But it's nice to know I can sometimes.

The last chapter ??? Wednesday, 25 June 7.00 PM

From: cassandra briggs [mailto: cassab88@yahoo.co.uk]
To: Jennings, Emma
Chapter 46.CB.doc

Hi Em
Yes, I was surprised when you hugged me. But I sort of caught your excitement. If you're not careful, you might have to stop saying 'I don't do hugs'!
Now I feel like I have to finish our story – especially while I'm feeling really good for almost the first time since the accident.
It has so helped me to get this down on paper. My psychologist called it 'a very successful cathartic exercise'. I think she means we've worked stuff out!! ☺
And the prom was awesome!!! I can't wait to see the official photos. Thank you so much for making me go – even if you were a real bully! Apparently Mum waited by the phone all evening, expecting me to ring her.
Must leave this now – someone's texting me . . .
Love
Cass xx

46

by Cass

You had to stay backstage. I think that was to help with someone else's props, was it? While you were doing that, I went in at the back of the hall to watch the rest of the performances. None of the other dances was as good as yours.

I couldn't wait to see you after they had finished. I went outside while Miss Tibbetts was saying something at the end.

I was hanging about in the playground like some groupie, waiting for you. I rushed up as soon as you came out of the door by the cloakroom where you'd been getting changed.

"You were amazing, Em – your dancing was fantastic."

Sorry if that sounded really gushy, but I was so impressed with what you had just done, I didn't really know what to say. I could feel the excitement rising up in me. Then you totally embarrassed me:

"It was your poem though, Cass. That just helped me through step-by-step. It gave me the beat, beat, beat." You moved your shoulders as you said this, in time to an imaginary rhythm. We both laughed.

"But your moves – it was like you were injected with electricity or something – it was astounding! That poem was just a bit of a rhyme. It wasn't exactly clever stuff. The way you danced to it was what made it work."

"You know Cass, I just love dancing. I felt sort of energised. I felt like me, the true me. Those words about longing, they just sort of wrapped round me."

You saying that made me think about how I used to feel when I was singing. When I was sure that was all I wanted to do all my life.

"You are a dancer, Em – that's who you are, that's who you'll always be."

"And you're the singer and poet of course. Maybe you'll be a singer/songwriter. That poem was well catchy."

I made a face at you, but didn't argue. Songwriter, maybe, but singer, oh, I don't know. But this wasn't the time to be negative. You caught hold of my hands and started to recite the long verse from my rhyme – much better than I did for the recording. I tried to pull away, but you held tight, making me move forwards and back, creating arches with my arms and swinging me around as you started to say . . .

"The shaping of my life
Is the feeling of the words,"

I joined in –

"Is the spirit of the dance
To the sounding of the beat
And the sharing of the soul
With the shaping of the space
For the changing of the whole
And the soaring of my mind
To the rhythm of the beat . . . beat . . . beat . . ."

Still we were laughing. You took off on your own and I tried another shorter verse

"But the dreaming of the dance
Is the longing of my life
And my coming close to You
To the rhythm of the beat . . . beat . . . beat."

I started to remember when I was writing the poem in our youth group. I now felt strangely closer to God and more sure of myself than I had even then. A crowd had gathered around us as the hall emptied. I noticed most of the parents were heading towards their cars, but all our lot involved in the performance were joining us. I saw Jock push his way forward and start to sway by you, his arms held high above his head as he began to clap, encouraging all the others to join in. You might not have noticed, but several girls, including Polly, had started to copy your moves. I reached the last line of the next stanza and I was amazed by the number of people joining me, shouting it out –

"To the rhythm of the beat . . . beat . . . beat." The voices carried on, and I heard new forms of my poem, shaped and altered – shouted out lines that fitted, really fitted. I just stopped and listened. It was an incredible, disorganised, rhythmic, wonderful noise.

I felt a hand on my shoulder. Without even thinking, I turned. Rob smiled at me.

"Are you the cause of all this commotion, Cass?"

"Only a bit," I said, smiling back, not caring that he could see my face, "it's Em's fault, mostly."

There was a lull in the chanting as people ran out of words – the mood was quietening, slowing down. It was just beginning to rain, very lightly. You slowed your dance, looking at me. I understood. Trying to feel not too self-conscious about Rob's hand, which was still resting lightly on my shoulder, I quietly carried on with the last verse as everyone stopped dancing except for you, Em.

"But the dreaming of the dance
Is the longing of my life
And my coming close to You
For the sharing of our souls
To the rhythm of the beat . . . beat . . . beat . . ."

As your dance finished, and the last 'beat' faded away, so everyone dispersed, back into their little groups of friends, or hurrying to their parent's cars. That just left you and me, Jock and Rob standing there, looking at each other. Smiling stupidly. Jock turned to face you. The way he was looking at you made me feel we shouldn't be there.

I felt Rob's hand leave my shoulder and touch my arm.

"Come on, Cass, I'll walk back with you, if that's all right?"

So he did.

Saturday, 28th June

Windows Live Messenger

Em the Gem says:
We did it!! J J

Cass X says:
Yep – just about finished.

Em the Gem says:
We can't really write anymore. We're up 2 date.

Cass X says:
Xept we haven't written about prom.

Em the Gem says:
What's 2 write? It was awesome. I danced all evening with Jock.

Cass X says:
I just danced with the crowd.

Em the Gem says:
Only cos Rob was playing. He was looking at u all the time.

Cass X says:
He's a friend.

Em the Gem says:
Oooooo – more than that I think

Cass X says:
Don't b silly! We just had gr8 chat on way home u no – God,

the Universe and everything.

Em the Gem says:
Easy to talk to is he?

Cass X says:
Yes. We're friends – like the same things. What about you + Jock?

Em the Gem says:
I'm really happy for first time in ages. Happy!!! So Happy!! ☺ ☺ ☺

Cass X says:
U no, I think I am 2 !! ☺

Em the Gem says:
We don't need 2 write more stuff, do we?

Cass X says:
Don't think so. My flashbacks & nightmares almost gone. R urs?

Em the Gem says:
Yes, xept 4 one in church hall. I let it come & go. I feel sane again, sort of.

Cass X says:
Sort of?

Em the Gem says:
Can't stop thinking about Jock!!!!! ☺

Cass X says:
Normal insanity, I think! Shall we stop writing?

Em the Gem says:
Ok. Then write a bit more if we ever need 2.

Cass X says:
Sounds good.

Em the Gem says:
Bit random, Jock thinks we ought 2 go out as 4some 2nite.

Cass X says:
Who's the 4th?

Em the Gem says:
Jock just asked Rob!

Cass X says:
What?????!!

Em the Gem says:
Rob said 'Brill' & he'd text u.

Cass X says:
I'll check mob. Oh, he did. What have u got me in2?

Em the Gem says:
Don't worry, b gr8. New opportunity!!.

Cass X says:
ok, ok – r we still doing that pact?

Em the Gem says:
Absolutely. C u l8r then? Meet here at 7?

Cass X says:
ok you bully!! C u l8r. J Bye 4 now.

Em the Gem says:
Bye! ☺

Acknowledgements

Thank you to Sherry Ashworth for her wisdom and guidance. Also my thanks go to all my readers and advisors for their valuable comments on the manuscript: Steph Richardson, Debbie Lu, Megan Taylor, Ian Nettleton, Sarah Hobday (the adults) and Jos, Rachel, Ellie, Rosalind and Hannah (the young adults). Thank you also to Ken who has proofread and looked after me while I attended to the demands of two emotional emailing characters.

www.annie-try.blogspot.com

www.annie-try.co.uk

ROUNDFIRE
BOOKS